A forceful man . . .

"There is nothing to discuss. I have made up my mind," he shot back, never losing a step. He could not keep from smiling at her distress, knowing that in a few minutes she would be furious again. He walked past the bed and directly into his dressing room. Joslyn did not have time to form a question before he tossed her onto the couch along the side wall. Then he turned on his heels and walked out.

Joslyn's legs were tangled in her skirt. She was still struggling to stand up when she heard the door close and the key turn in the lock. Scrambling to her feet, she ran to the door and tested the latch. It would not move.

"Devon, what have you done?"

"The honorable thing, love. Now get some sleep," he called through the door. "We shall have a nice long talk in the morning."

The Reluctant Suitor

Sarah Eagle

JOVE BOOKS, NEW YORK

THE RELUCTANT SUITOR

A Jove Book / published by arrangement with
the author

PRINTING HISTORY
Jove edition / July 1991

ISBN: 0-515-10610-0

Jove Books are published by The Berkley Publishing Group,
200 Madison Avenue, New York, New York 10016.
The name "JOVE" and the "J" logo
are trademarks belonging to Jove Publications, Inc.

PRINTED IN THE UNITED STATES OF AMERICA

10 9 8 7 6 5 4 3 2 1

To
KATHIE SEIDICK
and
GINA WILKINS,
this is your fault.

1

"HUSH, Ann-Louise, or we shall be caught," Joslyn Penderton admonished the whimpering bundle of fur in her arms as she straddled the window ledge of the sitting room's side window. The quivering thirty pounds of springer spaniel in her arms only made the difficult task worse. Climbing out the window in a dress would have been hazardous enough, even with her skirt pulled through her legs and secured by her sash. Now her beloved pet wanted to play coward. "I should just leave you here to the tender mercies of Aunt Verity's well-shod foot."

The threat seemed to quiet the year-and-a-half-old dog, who still thought she was a newly weaned puppy, while her mistress occupied herself in getting out the window without mishap. The midnight flight could have been accomplished by merely leaving through the front door or the kitchen or even the French windows in the dining room; however, Joslyn felt it lacked the proper spirit. By simply walking out the door, she would have lowered her leave-taking to a mundane occurrence. She was a young lady of twenty years of age, quickly approaching one and twenty, so this must be an event of adventure, not to be reduced to a juvenile start by improper execution. It was already a great disappointment that she was forced to wear a dress since she did not have the more proper disguise of male clothing.

Unfortunately her slender figure would have been dwarfed

by any of the available male apparel. Uncle Otis and Cousin Gervais outweighed her two or three times over, and she could not bring herself to pilfer from Atkins, the butler and general factotum, who had little to call his own. He had come to them with barely a shirt on his back, after losing his arm at Corunna two years before, and her mama had taken in the former soldier because of her beloved but absent husband's occupation in His Majesty's army.

Hot tears stung Joslyn's eyes at the thought of Papa, gone to his reward these past five months. Blinking away the unwanted moisture, she hopped down from the window and awkwardly picked up her bandbox. Ann-Louise whined her displeasure at the jostling and jolting she was experiencing in the usually comforting arms of her owner.

"Hush, now. I shall put you down when we are far enough away from the house," Joslyn commanded in an authoritative but sympathetic tone. Ann-Louise always flew into a frenzy of barking and jumping whenever her leash came into sight. Joslyn did not dare bring out the leather lead until they were out of earshot, or the dog's playfulness would wake the entire countryside. She had no other choice but to bring Ann-Louise with her for the escape, since the pampered liver-and-white-colored spaniel would refuse to eat without Joslyn present.

Though she knew the way to her destination well, Joslyn blessed the full moon. The brightness of the evening sky removed any of her apprehensions at the rustling in the bushes and unfamiliar noises around her. She crossed the expanse of the lawn in rapid strides to reach the woodlands that surrounded the house in a wide horseshoe pattern. Once she reached the shelter of the trees, she made for the log she had used as a refuge so many times in the past.

Ann-Louise cooperated until her mistress sat down heavily on the natural bench. Then she began squirming again in earnest to be released. The pair continued to battle until Joslyn pulled the leash from its hiding place. As she anticipated, her pet growled and let out a series of excited barks as the leather strap was secured at her collar. The animal sprang to the ground the second she was allowed, jumping and barking at nonexistent enemies. When no opponent materialized, she attempted to play tug-of-war with her leash, but discovered her mistress was not paying her the least attention.

"Oh, Ann-Louise, why did Papa have to die?" Joslyn asked, her earlier tears returning as she remembered the sad event that had brought her to this moment. She had not cried since the news first arrived; there had not been time when Mama went into a decline. Joslyn had to take charge while Lady Amelia mourned the loss of her husband, shutting herself away from the world in her room, eating little and speaking to no one.

A consoling whine brought Joslyn out of her dark study. She focused on her beloved pet—a gift from her father on his last trip home—now sitting obediently at her feet. Ann-Louise stared up at her mistress in confusion, with her head cocked to the side. Joslyn sighed, wishing that her conversations with her canine companion were not so one-sided.

"Come on, you *shtupid* beast, we still have a short way to go." Joslyn got reluctantly to her feet and pulled her hem free from her sash, allowing the dress to fall to her ankles. She set out with her bandbox in one hand and Ann-Louise's leash held firmly in the other. The dog trotted happily in front of her, satisfied with her lot now that she had four feet on the ground again. "You shall need to be on your best behavior. Margate is not going to be happy with us, and we want him to loan us his horse and cart."

Ann-Louise would not be worried about the ire of the Pendertons' former butler, since he always had a spare bone for her when she visited his cottage. Joslyn knew better. Margate was sure to lecture her on the foolishness of running away. He would not think the curse of her father's will a reasonable excuse for her flight, even with the added incentive of a prolonged visit from her Aunt Verity and her family.

"How could Papa do this to me? He promised I could decide my own future and not marry if I did not wish it," Joslyn explained for possibly the hundredth time, not caring that she was addressing trees, a disinterested owl, and other nocturnal animals. As the only child of General Sir Quentin Penderton and Lady Amelia, she was used to solitary pursuits. During her youth there had always been exciting places to see when Papa found his family a comfortable house wherever he had been posted, and Mama dithered about, wringing her hands. When Joslyn turned fourteen, she was sent to school at Miss Dempster's to be given the polish of a genteel young lady. She had then returned home to take over the running of the house—with her mama's full approval—that Papa built especially for his declining years.

Joslyn sniffed again at the melancholy thought that Papa would never spend those happy years he anticipated in the pretty red brick house. He was buried in a place called Fuentes de Onoro. The granite marker behind the house sat over an empty grave.

The sight of Margate's stone and thatch cottage over the crest of the hill forced Joslyn to compose herself. She had to face the old man with composure and a clear head, because he would undoubtedly try to sway her from her course. By the time she reached the cottage, Joslyn was ready to do battle. She rapped sharply on the rough wooden door. Her wait was not long; a light flickered in the darkness, and she could hear Margate's halting steps approaching.

"Who goes there?" called the old man, his gruff voice muffled by the wooden barrier.

"It is Joslyn. Let me in."

Immediately the bolt was released, and the door swung inward to disclose Margate's tall, thin form. He stood squarely in the doorway barring her entrance, holding a lantern in one hand and a pistol in the other. Raising the lamp, he gave her stiff-backed stance a thorough inspection, his eyes narrowing at the sight of her bandbox and Ann-Louise at her side.

"You're running away, are you?" he stated more than questioned, but stood aside to allow her entrance.

Joslyn walked quickly past him, her chin stuck defiantly in the air. She should have come in the daytime to make her request. No man liked to have his sleep disturbed or be caught in his nightshirt and cap, especially a man with Margate's temperament.

"Sit yourself down by the fire while I fetch my breeches, young miss, and then you can explain this latest start, or at least you can try," she was told none too gently before he disappeared into the next room. Joslyn did exactly as she was told, not wanting to antagonize him any more than necessary. Her idea had seemed so simple, so reasonable, until she'd met with the disapproving frown on the old man's face. Margate's ominous "young miss" told her she would have to suffer a minor skirmish in order to accomplish her task.

"Don't you have the brains you were born with, girl? You could've built up the fire while you waited, not sat here in the dark," Margate grumbled, stepping over Ann-Louise to stir up the glowing embers in the large stone fireplace.

"You told me to sit, so I did," Joslyn returned petulantly. If she had built up the fire, he would have complained of that as well.

The man only grunted in reply while adding more wood to the fire. Once he was satisfied with the blaze, he seated himself on the high-backed bench across from his visitor. "Now, what brings you here like a sneak-thief in the dark of night?"

"I thought it advisable to take a brief sojourn away from home at this time," Joslyn stated in a prim voice, and sat up as straight as she possibly could in a rocking chair. She met the iron-haired man's narrowed gaze without blinking, hoping she looked imposing, if not convincing. It was so hard to persuade a man who had carried her piggy-back as a child that she was grown up enough to make her own decisions.

"You are running away," Margate returned, nodding his head for emphasis, "and you know it's wrong, judging from that missish tone of yours. The general must be spinning in his grave at having such a cowardly child."

"I am not a child or a coward." She restrained herself from stamping her foot to prove her point. "I am simply retreating for the time being. But what if I am running away? It is Papa's fault."

"Ah, so you've heard from your betrothed then? Is that what has you behaving like a Bedlamite?"

"No, I have *not* heard from that man Papa foisted on me in his will. He does not seem to be any more interested in me than I am in him," Joslyn informed Margate with a sniff of disdain. Just a fortnight had passed since the general's new will had been read—the one he had written on the eve of the battle that had taken his life. After the shock of receiving his possessions some four months after his death—and Lady Amelia's third or fourth decline—the will had been discovered in Papa's trunk. Joslyn still felt an ache in her heart over his betrayal when the solicitor read . . . *and my beloved Joslyn's future is secured by bestowing her hand into the keeping of my noble aide, Captain Farraday, who shall provide for her and cherish her.*

"How could Papa do it, Margate? He promised me I would not have to marry if I truly did not wish it. He knew as soon as I reached one and twenty, I would have Grandmother's inheritance to keep me in a comfortable living." Joslyn gazed in confusion at the old man who had always comforted her in her darkest moments. Her shoulders began to droop in defeat at his implacable expression. She should have known he would not go against the general. He had been Papa's batman during the American rebellion, and when he had lost his leg at Yorktown, Papa had sent him back to England to serve his family.

"The general also knew you planned to go to London with some hare-brained notion about fancy parties, or some such nonsense."

"It is not nonsense. I am going to have a place in society for the military wives. The quality of the *ton* look down their collective noses at women who marry officers, almost as if they had the pox." She defended her plans immediately, though she and Margate had argued over this countless times before. "You saw how they treated Mama, and she the daughter of a baron. Well, I shall provide a place for our friends to have their own select society. Dances, soirees and musicales for the ladies while their husbands are off fighting for their country."

"Miss Joslyn, you've had only one trip to London to make your judgment on this. Your society folks aren't much different than the military. Each has its ranks." Margate gave a weary sigh and reached for his clay pipe from the box that hung by the fire. Taking down the tinder box as well, he took his time lighting the pipe. "Everyone isn't going to be equal, even if those Frogs have cut off the heads of everyone they disliked. Some will always fare better than others."

"I just want the military wives to have a choice. They need a leader to show them how it is to be done. I shall be like Madame de Stael, a gracious hostess opening my home—"

"Don't you start on that woman again. The only smart thing you've done since you read about her is name your dog after her," Margate broke in before Joslyn could begin on her favorite topic. "Tell me why you came here tonight, if you haven't heard from the captain."

"I am going away until after my birthday. It is only a few weeks away, and I can stay at Papa's hunting lodge until then." She began twisting the ribbons on her dress the moment Margate rolled his eyes at her plan. "I want to borrow your cart and horse because it is too far to walk, and I shall need transport to take in supplies. I just could not stay at the house a moment longer, waiting for that man to show up."

"The visit from your aunt and her family doesn't have a thing to do with it then? That would have sent *me* to parts unknown after the first day."

"Yes, well, Aunt Verity has been very sympathetic. She was horrified that I was to marry a man I did not know," Joslyn said, giving him a questioning look.

"Still wants you to marry her spotty son, does she? I'm betting his hands are still sweaty and his father is drinking himself under the table every night," he returned with a frankness that only servants with many years of service possessed. After almost thirty years with the Penderton family, he had been happy to retire to his cottage and tend a few sheep with the help of a boy from the village. He kept a proprietary eye on his ladies, however, even after training Atkins. Now that the general was gone, he knew he had to redouble his efforts and make sure young Joslyn was settled with a husband to contain her more spirited ideas.

"Yes, the Hunnycotes have not changed much since their last visit. Aunt Verity's been pushing Gervais forward as usual," Joslyn agreed with a dispirited sigh. "I suppose she thinks no one but Gervais would want to bother with me, if Captain Farraday had not been forced on me. Perhaps that is why the captain has not made an appearance. He knows he has been saddled with a bespeckled, brown-haired runt for a wife."

"You know better than to believe anything that sharp-nosed aunt of yours says, young miss. She's still jealous that your mother captured a general, and she had to settle for that fat merchant of hers. He was her only hope," Margate said forcefully at the girl's dejected look.

For years her aunt had badgered Joslyn about her looks. Joslyn was never going to be beautiful or have the delicate prettiness of her mother. Instead, she had appeal—a sweetness that struck a responsive chord in the male of the species. It had caused the old man to lose many a night's sleep since she began to blossom into womanhood. The young men in the surrounding villages were always falling over themselves to perform some small service for Miss Penderton. Joslyn simply took their attentions in stride because the Penderton household had been overflowing with officers during the peace of her early childhood when the general was stationed in England.

Joslyn was not aware of any masculine interest. She thought her halfpenny-bright curls were mousy and plain. Night after night she tried creams and lotions to remove the golden sprinkle of freckles on her button nose. Though she refused to stay out of the sun and frequently forgot her bonnet, Joslyn longed for her mother's flawless, milk-white complexion, never realizing her tawny skin brought out the color of her moss-green eyes. In his more fanciful moments, the general had likened her to a wood nymph straight from the pages of *A Midsummer Night's Dream*.

No, Margate decided, she was not going to be wasted on the likes of her idiot cousin Gervais. The general wanted his daughter to marry Captain Farraday, and Margate would see to it. He would merely have to keep her out of harm's way until the young man made an appearance. He knew nothing about the captain—the general's will was as much of a shock to him as it had been to the ladies—but, if the general approved of the man, that was good enough for Margate.

"Margate, you have not gone to sleep on me again, have you?" Joslyn's soft query broke into his rambling thoughts just as he came to a decision.

"No, Miss Joslyn, I was considering whether we should leave now or wait until the morning."

"We should what?" Joslyn could not keep her voice from coming out in a squeak of sound. Not once in all her planning and plotting had she imagined that Margate would be so cooperative.

"Tonight, I think," he continued, as if she had not spoken a syllable. "We'll hitch up old Cornwallis now, since half the night's gone already. The hunting lodge is less than an hour's drive, so we'll have a few hours sleep before we attempt making the place habitable in the morning."

"You are going with me? Truly?" Joslyn exclaimed, clapping her hands together in delight. This was beyond belief. Not only was Margate not going to send her home, but he was also going to accompany her. This was going to be a wonderful adventure after all.

Two days later Joslyn still had not lost her high spirits. She had escaped, and she was free. The thought caused laughter to bubble up inside her, as it had every time she considered her lot. Even Margate's grumbling while they scrubbed out the hunting lodge and put it to rights did not dampen her spirits. Today she left him muttering over rabbit stew for their dinner, while she took Ann-Louise out for a run.

The uncharacteristic dry and clear September day made her want to skip and dance. She did not have a care in the world. She had managed to escape from her unwanted fiancé as well as her cousin Gervais' attentions, and soon she could claim her inheritance to live as she wanted in London. The scheme would be simple. Mama knew she was in safe hands with Margate to protect her, and Joslyn would visit the solicitor in Manchester, collect her money and take the next coach—perhaps by a circuitous route—to London. Naturally, she would have to live under an assumed name in London, in the event that Captain Farraday finally decided to fulfill his duty to his former commander.

"What should it be?" she asked the nearest tree, pondering her new name with her arms spread and executing a graceful spin. Before she could think of a single choice, a loud bark from Ann-Louise brought Joslyn out of her daydream. The spaniel had bounded ahead of her earlier, and Joslyn had been allowing her to run off her excess energy so the young dog would be happily exhausted when they returned to the lodge, thus eliminating one item from Margate's list of complaints. Ann-Louise barked again, the sound coming from beyond the tangled hedgerow.

"You *shtupid* hound, are you challenging something smaller than yourself this time, or have you taken on yet another beast twice your size?" Joslyn muttered. She did not waste time speculating and picked up the skirt of her muslin dress so she could run easily over the uneven ground.

"Oh, dear," she exclaimed the second she wiggled through the shrubbery that bordered the roadway. Ann-Louise had taken on an opponent more than twice her size—an opponent who was dressed in the height of fashion, from his bottle-green coat to his once highly polished top boots, and was lying unconscious in the roadway.

Yes, he was simply unconscious, Joslyn realized, letting out a relieved breath as she fell to her knees beside the young man. His chest was moving up and down, so he was breathing. "Ann-Louise, what have you done now?"

Joslyn looked around, unsure what she should do next. Her agitated gaze discovered a curricle a few yards away, leaning on its side with one wheel broken. The team that had been pulling it was standing quietly, though Ann-Louise was sniffing around the horses' feet. Joslyn whistled softly to summon her pet. One false move from the horses, and the silly dog would come to grief.

Her whistle brought a response from Joslyn's new companion as well. He groaned, rolling his head to the side and causing a few errant locks of raven-black hair to tumble onto his forehead. His eyes opened, but Joslyn did not think his dark brown gaze was focused on her. He frowned for a minute, blinking as if trying to see her. Then he gave her an unexpected smile and closed his eyes.

She had to get help. Joslyn knew she must fetch Margate, but she hesitated for a moment, allowing her eyes to run over the stranger's face. He must be ten years her senior, even though he looked rather boyish at the moment. Impulsively she reached out to stroke his square jaw and was surprised to find it slightly rough to her touch. He murmured incoherently at her soft caress. With even greater daring, she smoothed his mussed hair away from his high forehead, tangling her fingers in his silky mane.

Ann-Louise brought Joslyn to her senses with a sharp bark and an impatient poke of her nose to her mistress' arm. Joslyn felt the heat of embarrassment burning her cheeks. Her hoydenish behavior was being reprimanded. She scrambled to her feet and called her pet to heel, tethering the dog to the bushes while she ran back to the lodge for Margate. With the old man's help and transport of the cart, they would soon have her handsome stranger safe and sound at the lodge.

2

JOSLYN had to clutch the side of the door frame to catch her breath when she reached the lodge. She had run as fast as her skirts would allow, pelting through the woods and underbrush with little regard for her appearance and the sounds of ripping fabric. Her heart pounded in her ears with each rasping breath she took to ease her bursting lungs. She rested her hot cheek against the cool plaster of the wall.

"By St. Catherine, girl, what have you done now?"

Joslyn let out a croaking shriek at the sound of Margate's gruff voice coming from behind her. She spun around to find him standing there with an ax in one hand and a pile of kindling sticks balanced precariously on one arm. She knew immediately she looked a sight when he dropped the wood to the ground and raised his ax in a defensive manner, ready to take on whoever was responsible for her tattered condition.

"Tell me what's happened to you," he demanded in a dangerous snarl. His eyes turned to steely slits, and the criss-cross of wrinkles on his face deepened with his scowl.

Still out of breath, Joslyn waved her hands in front of her in denial, shaking her head vigorously to calm his temper. "Not me. Man on the road. Needs help," she finally managed. "Curricle turned over."

"Is he injured?" Margate's thin body slumped in relief. He bent and leaned the ax against the lodge wall without

taking his eyes off the agitated young woman in front of
him. She started to nod, then shrugged in confusion. Tears
came to her eyes because she could not answer him. The
image of the still body she had left in the roadway was too
clear in her mind.

"It is my fault. I let Ann-Louise run loose," she rushed
on to explain, in full command of her voice once again.
Hastily she wiped the back of her hand across her cheek to
check her unwanted tears. She was behaving like a baby,
which added anger to her already unsettled emotions.

"You're a sight, young miss. Stop your blubbering and
go fetch some bandages while I hitch up Cornwallis,"
Margate ordered, turning on his good leg and walking
toward the stable without waiting for a reply.

Joslyn blew her disordered curls out of her eyes. She
watched the old man's halting steps across the yard with her
hands on her hips, quickly forgetting in her exasperation his
readiness to defend her. The man was utterly impossible.
Cornwallis' whinny of greeting when Margate entered the
stable brought her out of her aggrieved stance. She lifted her
skirts and raced into the lodge.

She headed straight for the kitchen on the far side of the
great room. Skidding to a stop by clutching the wooden
worktable in the middle of the room, Joslyn looked around
for anything that would be of use. Within a minute, she
snatched up every dish cloth in sight and took Margate's
apron for good measure, then raced back out to the yard.

As she expected, the cart and horse were pulled up
directly in front of the doorstep. Margate gave her a
speaking look as she scrambled up beside him, then slapped
the reins before she had time to sit down. Neither of them
said a word.

The trip back to where she left the unconscious stranger
seemed to take an eternity as Joslyn squirmed in her seat.
While she had taken the short cut through the woods, the
cart was forced to stay on the road. Cornwallis had never
moved so slowly, as if his legs were mired down in cold
molasses. After seemingly endless miles of roadway, the
broken curricle came into sight at the bend in the road, with

a matched pair of chestnuts grazing disinterestedly before it.

"There it is, Margate, there it is!"

"I see it, missy, so where's this man?" he responded in his usual grumble as she clutched his arm and bounced up and down on her seat. "Just settle yourself down, or you'll spook poor Cornwallis."

The sight of the stranger's still body prevented Joslyn from making a scathing retort. She jumped down before Margate had pulled in the reins, not a particularly daring feat since they had been traveling at a snail's pace. Ann-Louise barked an excited greeting from where she was tied, as Joslyn dropped to her knees beside the man. He was muttering to himself once more, but still seemed to be unaware of his surroundings. He did not open his eyes when she laid a gentle hand on his arm.

"Now, how do you expect me to help this young buck while you're hovering over him like a broody hen?" Margate looked down at his young mistress with concern. The young man was quality, it was plain to see, and the silly girl was already feeling responsible for his injuries. There was no way to tell if the man was honorable or a wastrel until he regained his senses. From the tragic look Joslyn cast up at him, the old soldier knew he would have to be extremely vigilant in the coming days.

"Go and keep that fool dog quiet and let me see what's to be done," he ordered, pulling Joslyn to her feet none too gently.

"I have helped tend the sick in the village," she protested, unable to keep her eyes off the stranger.

"No young lady in my charge will be checking to see if a young strapping man has any broken bones."

Joslyn knew her cheeks were bright red in embarrassment. First a dog and now a servant had taken her to task for her forward behavior in less than a half hour's time. Pouting slightly, she shuffled over to where she had tethered Ann-Louise. She watched in silence as Margate awkwardly lowered himself to the ground, his wooden leg stretched out to the side. He would have cuffed her ears if she offered him the least assistance; when he wanted help, he asked for it.

Over the years, Margate had learned the special balance to compensate for his infirmity; an infirmity no one dared point out to him.

With sure and practiced hands the old man checked the stranger for any broken limbs. Joslyn hardly blinked while he worked. Ann-Louise whined and batted her mistress's hand with her wet nose, but Joslyn could not take her attention from the inert figure lying in the road. The stranger remained still, no longer turning his head from side to side and muttering unintelligible sounds. Margate grunted and hemmed and hawed.

Finally, Joslyn could not wait a second longer. "Well? Is he all right?"

"Yes, by some stroke of luck, he isn't damaged too badly. But I'm glad to see he's still out of his senses."

"Damaged?" The word came out in a squeak, and Joslyn took a quick step forward.

"He didn't break anything, but his shoulder is pulled out," the old man observed as though talking about the weather. "It will be easier to put back in place without him being aware of it."

"Put back?"

"Missy, if you're planning to repeat everything I say, I'll get Cornwallis to help me," Margate grumbled. "A fine time for you to start catching your mama's die-away airs. Come over here and help a crippled old man get on his pins."

Joslyn did as he bade her, with only a sniff of disdain in response. As she had learned to do from many years of practice, she made a brace of her arms, folding them in front of her, her hands clasped at her elbows, so Margate could steady himself against them as he staggered to his feet.

"We really are not going to . . . er, rearrange his shoulder, are we?" Joslyn knew it was an idiotic question from the hard look the old man gave her. She shivered as she waited for her next instructions. As the sun began to set, a cool breeze stirred in the gathering dusk, but that was not the cause of her discomfort.

"Yes, missy, we're going to rearrange his shoulder, and you will have to do the most important job."

"I do?"

"Come stand in front of me. Then bend down and slowly raise his arm without allowing it to bend. That's it, Miss Jos." Margate murmured the last encouragement when she looked questioningly over her shoulder. "Never mind if he groans, he can't really feel it. Now, bring it straight up while you stand."

"Margate, are you going to make me do something sickening?" Joslyn whispered her query without realizing it, hoping this was all he expected her to do.

"Yes, Miss Joslyn, but it would be much worse if he was awake and staring up at your every move," the old man stated, not reassuring her one whit. "The general and I did this too many times to count for those young fools they'd send up who had less sense than their mounts."

"What do I do now?" She clasped the stranger's wrist in her hand, his skin warm to her touch. Beneath her damp palm she could feel the steady beat of his pulse. It reassured her somewhat.

"Place your foot between his collarbone and the curve of his shoulder," Margate continued relentlessly. "That's it, and it will all be right as a trivet with just a little tug."

Before Joslyn knew what he was about, the old man put his arms around her from behind and covered her hands with his own. Suddenly he pulled sharply upward, causing the stranger to cry out at the jarring movement.

"That should do him nicely," Margate observed, stepping back and dusting off his hands in satisfaction. "Hold on there, missy, don't go fainting on me now that we're only half done. We still have to get him in the cart."

Joslyn stiffened her drooping spine and whirled around to confront the old man. "That was disgusting, you odious old man. I could feel his shoulder pop under my foot."

"There wasn't another way. If I had tried it alone, I'd be flat on my back in the dirt, and he'd still be in pain," Margate returned, his gray eyes apologetic, but a stern glint told her he would have made her do it all over again if necessary. "The worst is over, missy. We only have to strap his arm to his chest. That'll keep it from jostling when we put him in the cart."

Joslyn never admitted it, but the worst was over. Under Margate's instructions, she knelt at the man's head and lifted him gently so Margate could cut away his coat and shirt. She was appalled that they were destroying such fine cloth, but knew it had to be done since they could not bind his arm when he was fully clothed.

It was not the first time she had seen a man without his shirt, though never one at such close proximity, or one so smooth and tautly muscled. In fact, she couldn't remember seeing a man's bare chest since she was a young child. His head rested on her shoulder while Margate used the man's shirt to secure his arm. The stranger was very quiet now, and Joslyn was surprised to see a smile on his face.

Another hour passed before they had the man settled in Sir Quentin's field bed at the lodge, the only bed suitable for the invalid. Sir Quentin often used the old mortar and timber lodge as a bolt hole after a few days of his family's loving attentions when on leave. There were the basic creature comforts, but little else; he had been a man of simple tastes.

After all her activity, Joslyn could barely stay awake over Margate's excellent rabbit stew. She looked in on the stranger one last time before going in search of her own bed, and Margate went to tend the horses. Her first look in the mirror jarred her out of her near slumberous state. Her curls stuck out haphazardly, a few pieces of leaves and a twig adding to the jumbled coiffure. There was a smudge across her forehead and down one cheek.

Her concern for the stranger had made her forget all else. A scattering of freckles had blossomed across her snub nose in the late afternoon sun. She looked no better than any of the village children after a strenuous game of fox and geese.

Joslyn wrinkled her nose and stuck out her tongue at her reflection. She was being a goose to worry about her appearance. The young man had been unconscious almost from the moment she found him. The one time he opened his eyes, he probably had not actually seen her due to the pain in his shoulder. What mattered was that she and Margate had been able to help the man. She had been on a mission of mercy, not promenading at a fancy dress ball.

With a resigned sigh, Joslyn turned away from the mirror and carefully removed her dress. At any other time she would have consigned the garment to the rag pile, but she did not have that luxury at the lodge. Her wardrobe was very limited, so tomorrow she would have to mend the dress as best she could. She would need some quiet activity while taking her turn in the sick room, she decided, pulling her serviceable cotton nightdress over her head.

Humming to herself, she brushed out her tangled curls, making sure all the residue of the woods were removed. She scrubbed her face and hands, then quickly climbed into bed—not disturbing the sleeping lump at the foot that was Ann-Louise—with the happy thought of adding to her adventure on the morrow. Maybe the stranger was running away, too, or perhaps he was . . . Joslyn drifted off to sleep still considering what exotic background her stranger would have.

He opened his eyes, his mind fuzzy, trying to see in the gloom that surrounded him. Blinking rapidly to clear his vision, he moved restlessly, then tensed in surprise. He could not move, and his entire body ached. With an effort he tried to raise his head, only managing to shift on the soft cushion beneath his head. He knew he was alarmed by what was happening, and knew he should know the cause for it, but he could not remember what brought him to this circumstance.

A strange sound broke the stillness of what he was sure must be the dead of night. He rolled his head in the direction of the sound. By narrowing his eyes he could make out the shape of a door, the outline becoming more distinct from a light coming from behind it. The sound was footsteps, irregular steps as if the person were favoring one foot as he walked across the wooden floor.

The door creaked open. A tall, thin man stood in the

opening with a candlestick in one hand. For a moment he hesitated while the dim light shone on the solitary figure in the bed. "Ah, you're awake then, young man."

The young man did not say a word or move a muscle. He blinked against the sudden light to allow his eyes to adjust, not daring to move due to the aching of his entire body and the pounding pain in his head. Instead he watched his visitor walk with an uneven, stiff-legged gait to his bedside. At closer range he could see the man was at least sixty years of age, with a face that was stern but not sinister.

"Where am I?" he asked as the older man sat down by the bed and reached over to unbind the strap that was holding the patient in bed.

"You're at Penderton Lodge. We found you in the roadway this afternoon after you took a tumble from your curricle," the man explained in a gravelly voice. "My name is Margate."

The young man knew by his companion's inflection that he was expected to respond by giving his own name. He thought for a minute, but nothing came to him except an increased pounding inside his head. He moistened his lips and closed his eyes, hoping the action would bring back his memory. Then a small kernel of knowledge floated upward through the gray fog that was occupying his brain. "Devon. My name is Devon."

Feeling a great sense of accomplishment, he opened his eyes and smiled at the stern-faced Margate. The old man did not comment, but leaned to his side to pour a glass of water from the ironstone pitcher on the table next to the bed. He took a paper twist from his vest pocket and tore it open, pouring the powdered contents into the water.

"Drink this. It should help the hammering in your head. I won't pester you with any more questions tonight; God knows, you'll get enough of that tomorrow from Miss Joslyn."

"Miss Joslyn?" Devon asked, trying to sit up. What little strength he had was useless, especially with the discovery that his left arm was strapped to his chest. Looking down, he grimaced as he recognized the fine lawn bandage as remnants of his shirt. Now, why did he know that and could not remember if Devon was his first or last name?

Margate stood up and helped Devon sit up enough to drink from the glass. "Miss Joslyn found you on the road today. This is her lodge where you'll be staying for a bit, Mr. Devon. Your shoulder was dislocated, and you'll be feeling the fall for a few days."

"My horses? Are they all right?" Devon could not believe how weak he felt from the small exertion of sitting up. "And what was that you gave me?"

"You are a gentleman then, thinking of your horse flesh first before questioning a headache powder," Margate stated, his expression never changing.

"You sound like my batman—" Devon broke off when he could not remember the man's name. A narrow face with a hawk-like blade of a nose flashed through his mind, but that was all. He turned a pleading look toward the old man. "I cannot remember his name."

Margate's face was more animated, his bushy eyebrows raised and a slight smile turning up the edges of his thin mouth. "Don't worry yourself, Mr. Devon. You'll do better in the morning after a good night's sleep. I'd say you were a military man at some time. When you feel better, we can trade stories. I'll tell you the honest truth of the Americas, and you can tell how things have changed against the Little Dictator."

"Too much rain," Devon murmured as he closed his eyes again, "and too much mud." He could see faces in the darkness behind his eyes, but he could not name one of them. They were seated around a fire, laughing and passing a bottle. Devon did not hear Margate leave the room as he tried to remember who the men in his vision could be. Other images took their place, however, as he started to drift back to sleep.

Miss Joslyn Penderton. He knew that name from somewhere, but this time there was not a face to go with it—or was there? He had an image of a little girl with corkscrew curls playing with a hoop. That did not make sense. How could a little girl own a lodge? That was what Margate said, that Miss Joslyn owned the lodge. Another face took shape in the fog—a gamine face, with huge green eyes and a smudge on her soft cheek.

"The poor girl has such a delicate condition, and we thought it best to send her to Torquay for the sea air." Devon could hear the shrill voice as if the woman was in the room with him, but he could not remember who the thin, sharp-featured woman was talking about. He could see a pleasantly decorated sitting room with four people in it.

The woman to his right was talking, gesturing in large sweeping motions as she spoke. "The poor dear was grief-stricken over her dearest father's death. It was so like our sweet Cousin Selina when she lost her second baby, so inconsolable. Of course, she was never really right again, poor soul. They were always finding her wandering in the roadway, talking to fence posts or a milestone and asking about her baby. Not that our Joslyn is in such a condition. She just needs a little rest, and of course, a little time to get accustomed to the thought of marrying a stranger. That is so, is it not, Amelia?"

Amelia was seated on Devon's other side. She was a soft, round lady who had been pretty in her younger days. In Devon's thoughts she was past her prime and frightened of her own shadow, or so it seemed. Not once had her rounded green eyes met anyone else's in the room, finding the bottom of her teacup very stimulating. The sound of her name startled her so much that she spilled her tea. As she mopped it up with her plump fingers, she spoke in a breathless voice, "Oh, yes, that is so—rest and time."

Though he could see their faces and hear the conversation, he still could not remember the place or the occasion. There were two men in the room as well who looked like bookends—one young and the other old. Both were portly and short, slouching in their chairs as the hatchet-faced woman continued talking about the person they had sent away. Soon the older man fell asleep, lolling back in his chair and occasionally joining the woman's monologue by snoring loudly.

"Devon, my boy, you must take care of my Amelia and

my girl if I do not survive tomorrow's battle." The sitting room was gone, and in its place was the campfire Devon had seen earlier. There were tents scattered around them with other fires. Next to Devon was an older man, his uniform proclaiming him a general. Devon was also in uniform, a captain's uniform. The hawk-beaked man was stirring something in a pot over the fire.

Devon heard his own voice respond. "Yes, sir, I shall do my best to watch over them." Then the fire disappeared, and all he could remember was pain and men screaming around him. Just as quickly, the screams turned to laughter. Instead of wounded soldiers all around, there were men dining on beefsteak and wine.

"You don't really have to marry the girl, do you?" asked the man seated across the table from him. Devon knew the man well, but again could not put a name to a face. "Just take the trip up to Dukinfield and sound her out. See that the old boy's family is taken care of, and that will be that."

Suddenly an older man was standing by the table. Devon looked up, and for the first time in the foggy, disjointed recital he had a name to match a face. The man was Lord Stanhope, but he could not fathom why the man was taking the bother to speak to him. Devon only knew the member of the House of Lords from his days at Eton with his son.

"Ruston, did I understand you were traveling north?" the tall, stately gentleman asked, bowing courteously to pass over his interruption. "I have need of a man who would be traveling near Manchester and would be interested in undertaking a mission of great importance to his country."

Lord Stanhope faded into the fog just as the other images had, and another room materialized. Devon was in a tavern now, talking to the innkeeper. Above the noise of the public room across the hallway, he asked about the road conditions. "Well, gov'ner, there be a road that'll take miles offen your journey. Ya did say ya was headed for Man'ester, din ya?"

The beady-eyed publican faded into the shadows with the others, leaving Devon tooling down a country road, springing his horses. One minute he was smiling in appreciation of the clear sunshine of the day, and the next he was being catapulted into the air.

Devon awoke with a start. Something cold and wet was pressing against his arm. Daylight was streaming into the bedroom when he opened his eyes, erasing all the shadowy figures and voices of his dreams. The cold wetness moved against his arm. He jumped in surprise and immediately regretted the movement. Not only did he jolt the bruises from his fall the day before, but he also jarred the newly healed saber wound in his side. As he looked down, his gaze locked with a pair of expressive brown eyes. He was being scrutinized by a not-so-ferocious beast resting its head on the mattress with its curly-haired ears spread out over the sheet and its cold, wet nose pressed against his arm.

"Good morning," Devon said with as much friendliness as he could muster. Moving cautiously, he brought up his free hand, taking care not to startle the dog or jar his own body again. The animal gave his hand a delicate sniff and plopped its head down on the sheet again. Devon tentatively stroked the top of the dog's head, quickly finding the right spot to scratch behind the left ear. The dog showed its appreciation by closing its eyes and whimpering in pleasure.

"Ann-Louise, you naughty girl," exclaimed a feminine voice from the doorway. "The gentleman is sick. He is not here to attend to you."

"She is not a bother," Devon began, smiling reassuringly at Ann-Louise before looking up. His breath caught in his throat when he saw the young woman standing in the doorway holding a tray in her hands. She was the gamine-faced girl who had been in his dreams, only now in full possession of his senses and in the strong light of day, he could see she was a pretty young woman.

While she fussed at the dog as she placed the tray on the night table, Devon studied her face. She had the most startlingly green eyes he had ever seen—round and clear, surrounded by lush black eyelashes. Her skin was tawny rather than peaches and cream, but flawless just the same. Her rounded face with its snub little nose and freckles above a soft, rosy mouth was not remarkable. Then she turned and smiled at him, the sunlight seeming to gild her chestnut curls. Her eyes twinkled with secret amusement as if they shared a joke, and a single dimple appeared just below the right corner of her mouth. He had been rescued by a wood nymph.

"Are you feeling more the thing this morning, Mr. Devon?" she asked as she finally had to pull the dog forcibly from the side of the bed. "Margate said you slept through most of the night."

"Yes, yes, I am," he answered. He was still slightly dazed by her appearance, not sure how she had become part of his dreams.

"Good, your color is much better than when I found you yesterday lying in the road," she continued. "I have brought you some tea and bread pudding to help build up your strength."

Devon could not think of anything that sounded more unpalatable than bread pudding, and thought longingly of the rare beefsteak that had been before him in his dream. It was clear that this was the lady who found him yesterday. He had apparently been conscious at some point yesterday.

"Now, I have forgotten my manners. I am Miss Joslyn Penderton, and from what Margate says, you will be accepting our hospitality for a few days," she explained in a rush. She gave him a nervous look, then walked to the trunk at the end of the bed. Opening the camelback lid, she continued to babble, "I hope you find the lodge comfortable. My father used to come here to rusticate when he was on leave from the army, so we do not have very many luxuries."

Devon barely paid attention to her chatter. His memory, so faulty during the night and throughout his dreams, was now in excellent repair. He knew exactly who he was and, more importantly, he knew exactly who the young woman at the end of the bed was as well. This slender young creature was his betrothed, the young daughter of his late commander, Sir Quentin Penderton!

He felt almost as nonplussed as he had the day in the solicitor's office when he discovered just what he had promised the general on the night before the battle of Fuentes de Onoro. Devon had been wounded himself while carrying messages. He had been invalided home to recover his injuries. Once he recovered sufficiently, he had visited his solicitor on another matter, only to discover Sir Quentin's solicitor had written to London concerning his client's new will. Until that moment, Devon had thought the man's daughter was no more than twelve years of age, and he had agreed to act as executor of the will.

"Mr. Devon, are you all right? You look very pale."

Devon was jolted back to the present by her anxious query. Joslyn was standing beside his bed again with two pillows clutched in her arms. He wondered if her concerned expression would turn to anger, or abject horror, or delight if he introduced himself properly. What would she do if he stated very clearly that he was Devon Alexander Delane Farraday, Marquess of Ruston, her fiancé?

The other question that was uppermost in his mind was, what was the girl doing here? Her harpy of an aunt said the girl had been sent away because of her grief over her father's death. So why was Miss Joslyn not in Torquay and not showing any sign of inconsolable grief or madness? Had it only been a day since he had visited the Penderton home? Something was not right, although the girl's mother, Lady Amelia, had not seemed too upset by her daughter's absence, merely nervous.

Perhaps he was still dreaming, and he would wake up snug in his bed in Cavendish Square. He knew there was no hope for that, so he quickly determined his course. Mr. Devon would continue to visit at Penderton Lodge while his bruises healed, and he would be the judge of the condition of Miss Joslyn Penderton's mental capability.

3

"I am grateful you were visiting the lodge during my hour
of need," Devon stated, his tone even as his eyes were
trained on Joslyn's face. "And may I say I have never had
such a charming rescuer before this."

Joslyn could feel the heat of her blush rise rapidly from
the drab, high neck of her gray cambric dress, wishing that
she had chosen more attractive dresses for her flight from
home. She squeezed the two pillows in her arms tightly
against her chest and scolded herself for her foolishness at
being nervous. She had seen brown eyes before entering the
room. Ann-Louise had brown eyes. There was no earthly
reason why Mr. Devon's regard should make her heart skip
a beat, or make her blush such a fiery red.

Perhaps it was the excessive amount of bare, tanned chest
that he was displaying beneath his white bandages that was
the cause. Despite her lofty claims to Margate about tending
the sick, Joslyn had never seen a man stripped to the waist,
at least not since she was a child. If her memory served,
only her father, Margate, and old Treble who came to shoe
the horses could be used as a comparison. For a fleeting and
uncharitable moment, she almost wished Mr. Devon would
lapse into an unconscious state again.

"Are those pillows for me?" her unwitting tormentor
inquired, breaking into her agitated thoughts.

"Er, yes . . . um, yes, they are," Joslyn managed to

respond, her fingers plucking at the embroidered edge of
one of the pillow slips. She could feel her blush
deepening—if that were possible—as the corner of his
mouth seemed to twitch in amusement. "You will need to
be propped up further to eat."

Silence fell between them as Joslyn contemplated how
this was to be accomplished. Margate would never approve
of her helping Mr. Devon to sit up with any physical
contact. The old man made that clear this morning by telling
her how he expected her to behave around the invalid.
Unfortunately, Margate was out tending to the horses, and
she would not be able to call him for assistance. As she
struggled to find a solution, the patient was having a
struggle of his own by attempting to sit upright without any
assistance.

"Here, give me your hand, sir," she shot out, dismissing
Margate's instruction as fustian. She was not going to let the
man injure himself further while she worried over what was
proper.

With an economy of motion, Joslyn grasped his forearm
and pulled him to a sitting position with a gentle but steady
pressure. After a slight fumble, she placed the two extra
pillows behind him. She stepped back and gave her companion a grin of triumph at the accomplishment.

He returned her smile, and she was glad for the diversion
of picking up his breakfast tray, even if the crockery rattled
slightly, and placing it before him. It was not going to take
Margate's lecture for Joslyn to remember how to behave in
the presence of the injured gentleman. Mr. Devon had the
strangest effect on her composure, and his brilliant smile did
nothing to lessen the pounding of her heart.

"Now then, you seem to be settled, so I shall just go see
if Margate has retrieved your luggage," she said briskly.
With her hands clasped tightly in front of her and her spine
rigid, she felt she was a perfect pattern card of the calm and
collected young lady.

"Oh, do not leave." The deep-voiced request, sounding
almost wistful, caught Joslyn just as she turned away.

"Please, stay and talk to me while I partake of this interesting . . ."

Joslyn could not stop the giggle that bubbled up in her throat at his helpless expression while trying to graciously describe Margate's sickroom fare. "It is pap, I know. *I* had to eat porridge for breakfast with Margate watching. I'm sure he will allow you some real food by this evening, but only if you eat each and every last drop now, Mr. Devon."

"Miss Penderton, I bow to your superior knowledge of the gentleman, or at least I would if I thought I could stand up without falling over," Devon replied, dipping his head in a mock bow. "Please, bring a chair over here and tell me how you found me yesterday."

Joslyn obeyed his request, quickly forgetting her misgivings of a few minutes earlier. Somehow their shared commiseration over Margate's bullying had diminished her nervous reaction to this gentleman. Though his profile closely resembled the handsome image she had seen once on a Roman coin, he was human and had a sense of humor.

"I have to confess before you make any further speeches of gratitude," Joslyn said as she settled herself a respectable distance from his bedside, "I am responsible for your misfortune by letting Ann-Louise run free yesterday. I fear that she startled your horses."

"No, no, it was neither your fault nor your friendly pet's in startling my cattle. I was not giving proper attention to my handling of the ribbons when the wheel apparently hit a rut or a stone in the road," Devon answered quickly between spooning soggy bits of bread from his bowl. "I also must clarify something about my name. When I spoke to the venerable Margate last night, I could only remember a single name, Devon, which is my first name. I hope you would not think it odd if I ask to be called by Devon, rather than Mr. Delane?"

"I would be pleased to call you Devon, though Margate will undoubtedly scold me for it. In return, you must call me Joslyn," she said and relaxed even more under his friendly smile. Devon was not daunting at all, but a fellow conspirator against the taciturn retired butler. "I never quite know exactly who Miss Penderton could be. In the village, everyone calls me Miss Joslyn, which is much nicer and without any starch to it. Though I suppose when I go to London, I must become used to the ways of polite society."

"You are planning a visit to the city soon?" Devon placed his empty bowl on the tray, giving all his attention to her reply as he raised his cup of tea to his lips.

"Oh, yes, quite soon. I shall be one and twenty in a few weeks, and shall come into my inheritance. Then I shall go to London and follow the example of Madame de Stael," she stated with pride, sitting up straighter and holding her head up in her most regal pose. She did not discover if this was successful, however, since Devon choked on his tea at that moment. "Devon, are you all right?"

"Yes, Joslyn, do not fuss. I simply swallowed at the wrong moment," Devon assured her, placing his cup carefully into its saucer before putting his hands flat on the tray. "You are an admirer of Madame de Stael? Are you planning on taking up a pen to make your way in society?"

"Oh, heavens no. I suffer over simply writing a letter. I could never do anything so beautifully tragic as *Delphine*," Joslyn returned, letting out a regretful sigh at her lack of talent. "I mean to emulate Madame as a hostess in the grand style. I plan to have exclusive entertainments for the ladies of the military. I admire Madame greatly and even named Ann-Louise after her."

"Is your father in the King's service? I suppose that is what gave you the inspiration?"

"Papa was with Wellington at Fuentes de Onoro. Now that he's gone, I must make my own way, for Mama and myself," she explained, leaning forward in eagerness at having a new audience to hear her grand plan. Surely Devon would not say she was a hen-wit, or tell her the idea was preposterous. He appeared to be a man of the world, and had not laughed or sneered when she mentioned Madame's name. He was listening politely with a very earnest expression.

"There is not a gentleman you wish to marry?" he asked.

"I do not plan to marry. I shall be a woman of

independence," Joslyn stated with a defiant nod, dismissing the absent Captain Farraday without a second's thought.

"Madame de Stael again?" Devon was beginning to reconsider his earlier judgment. Perhaps the young woman was suffering from some mental aberration, and the grim Margate was her keeper. At first she seemed normal enough, until her statement about following the example of Germaine de Stael—hardly a noble undertaking—which had nearly caused his demise from a hearty swallow of tea. Either the young woman was suffering from a brain disorder, or was so incredibly innocent that she knew nothing of Madame's hedonistic lifestyle.

"No, though I admire Madame's ability in writing and her talents for entertaining, I simply want to be the one who determines the direction of my life," Joslyn said, her expression earnest and all signs of amusement gone from her green eyes. "Mama says it is because I spend too much time alone and reading books that fill my head with nonsense. Until recently, however, I thought Papa had supported my ideals."

"What—" Devon barely formed his question when he became aware of an ominous figure standing in the bedroom doorway. Margate's tall, thin form showed every inch of his disapproval, his face a hard mask that carved every wrinkle and line into deep creases.

Joslyn turned her head to follow the direction of Devon's preoccupied gaze. She sprang to her feet, paying no attention to the clatter of her chair when it hit the floor. Devon watched her profile in fascination. She was magnificent in her defiant stance, her chin thrust upward as she waited for the old man to speak. She was without a doubt the general's daughter. Devon had seen that imperious pose just before the eve of battle as Sir Quentin prepared to meet the enemy.

"Dev— Mr. Delane has just finished his breakfast, Margate. I hope you were able to fetch his curricle and salvage his belongings," Joslyn stated in a clear, level tone, all traces of the impish wood nymph gone from her face.

Devon silently congratulated her for the tactic of going for the offensive position against her opponent.

Margate narrowed his eyes, his malevolent gaze moving past his mistress to Devon's impassive face. "Yes, young miss, I've brought in the gentleman's belongings. If you would be so good as to take away his tray, I'll be checking his bandages and see that he is properly clothed for your next visit."

Joslyn gave the former butler a condescending inclination of her chestnut curls, though there was a telltale hint of color to her cheeks. Margate had managed to be both authoritative and servile with a few simple sentences. The young woman turned to Devon with a fixed smile, only rolling her eyes in exaggerated martyrdom when her back was to the disapproving servant. "Mr. Delane, if you feel more the thing later, perhaps we can continue our conversation, or possibly a game of draughts or chess will help while away the hours."

"Whatever would be the most convenient for you, Miss Penderton," Devon replied in kind, stressing her formal name. He made a show of rearranging the bedclothes when Joslyn removed his tray, then laid his hand on top of the comforter while he watched her leave the room. She glided out with a serene gaze, only giving away her true feelings when she reached Margate's imposing figure. He was forced to step aside to allow her passage. When this was accomplished, she passed him by with an audible sniff and a toss of her burnished ringlets.

Devon waited with a mixture of amusement and interest for Margate's next maneuver. He was more than familiar with the terrorizing ways of servants from Backworth, his valet, to his wiry little batman, Hachetts. Margate had the same look in his steely eyes as either Backworth or Hachetts when lecturing Devon on the negligence of his clothing.

Devon knew Margate's thoughts had taken a much more serious direction, however. Though how the man thought he could possibly seduce the girl in his condition, he could not fathom. Devon had been complimented a number of times on his abilities with the gentler sex, but even flirting was beyond his capability at the moment. He also did not lure innocents into the pleasures of the flesh, even if they were in full possession of their senses, which he still had not ascertained about Miss Joslyn Penderton.

"If you'll excuse my presumption, sir," Margate said from beside the bed, his expression proclaiming he was going to presume with or without permission, "Miss Penderton is already spoken for, and with her father's approval. Her betrothal will be officially announced very soon."

Devon waited patiently while the older man checked the tautness of the binding at his shoulder, flinching only once when the cloth pulled against a tender portion of his skin. He waited for the man to step back before he responded. "I should let you work yourself into a fine rage over the next few days, but I value my hide. Since I would not want to be permanently incapacitated for the rest of my life, I shall explain that my full name is Devon Alexander Delane Farraday."

Devon paused to allow the import of his name to sink in before he continued with his revelation. An anticipated, the result was all he could hope for as Margate's long jaw gaped open, and his arms hung limply at his sides. Devon wondered what his next bit of news would do, since the general's will had cited him simply as Captain Farraday. "I have recently been on medical furlough from the Peninsula and Penderton's Light Horse, but am usually named as the Marquess of Ruston."

"Sir," Margate said as he came out of his fatuous stupor with a click of his heels as soon as Devon mentioned Penderton's brigade. But his eyes narrowed again as Devon stated his title. "What was the general thinking of to shackle the miss to some fancy nob?" Margate said bluntly.

Devon was intrigued. Usually his uniform did not make the slightest impression, except with the ladies; it was only when his title was brought to the fore that toad-eaters fell over themselves. Yet here was a servant who found approval in the rank of captain and nothing pleasing in the peerage. He wondered if Margate even knew he had spoken his question aloud.

"If you would take a seat, my good man, we have a number of things to discuss, not forgetting the stories of the Colonies that you promised me last evening. Put yourself at ease," Devon invited, making sure to keep his tone genial. He wanted to learn a few things from the old man before he gave him a full budget of what had brought him to this unexpected pass. Lord Stanhope had urged secrecy on his mission to Manchester. Devon would keep his own counsel on that issue, unless he felt it necessary to involve either the old servant or his charming betrothed.

Margate righted the chair that Joslyn toppled in her leave-taking. With a flick of his wrist, he turned its ladder back toward the bed, and taking Devon at his word, straddled the seat with his wooden leg stuck out to the side and his arms folded across the back. "I don't understand what's brought you here. Lady Amelia hasn't the power of logical thought to have discovered Joslyn's whereabouts so soon."

"So, the girl has not been gone that long on her trip to Torquay for the restorative effects of the sea air," Devon mused. He raised a single eyebrow in question for Margate to continue his involuntary confession.

"You've been to the house then, have you? Should I hazard a guess that you spent most of the visit listening to Verity Hunnycote?" At Devon's nod, Margate continued to speculate. "So, the miss is in need of restorative measures, but not due to a visit from her harpy aunt or her sot of a husband and her spotty son, I'll wager. What was the cause?"

"Her grief over the general's death. It seemed to affect her the same way as some relative who talked to fence posts, I was led to believe," Devon answered with an effort at keeping his face suitably impassive for the seriousness of the ailment. "How dangerous is the girl? Does she bay at the moon in the dark of night, or simply talk to inanimate objects as an inherited trait?"

"Bosh, if anyone's daft, it's that sharp-nosed aunt of

hers. Miss Joslyn behaves foolishly at times, but she's as right as a trivet." Margate's fierce scowl had returned as he thought of how his mistress was being maligned. "The general wouldn't have wanted the girl to marry if she was addlepatted. Now, mind you, there are times she's a trifle impetuous, but she's sound."

Devon resisted the urge to ask about her teeth and fetters, knowing the other man was not aware he was making his charge appear to be a filly on the block at Tattersall's. "Margate, this whole situation has put me into a bit of a quandary over what is to be done," Devon began without any real idea of where his ramblings would take him. "You see, I thought I was agreeing to be the executor of the general's will for his very young daughter. Unfortunately, neither of us thought the need for my services would be necessary so quickly, but I find myself engaged to a young woman who has no desire to marry."

"Miss Joslyn has a very short-sighted perspective of the real world, m'lord. And though I hate to agree with anything her aunt has to say, it's true that the miss hasn't fully recovered from the shock of the general's will." Margate paused and rubbed his jaw with bony fingers, his calculating gaze running over the man on the bed. "She's run away to avoid meeting this Captain Farraday. Though I think she's a bit peeved that he hasn't shown any interest in making her acquaintance. Of course, having her relatives move in would send anyone running to the hills."

"I think we need to continue with keeping my real identity a secret between the two of us. Until I can determine the means to resolve this delicate situation, Joslyn will simply help nurse her new friend Mr. Delane back to health," Devon instructed. He hoped he was mistaken in the gleam he saw in the old man's eyes. The look was too close to the acquisitive expression of all the fond mamas at Almack's when pushing their daughters forward with any eligible partee. "Now that that is settled for the time being, how did you find my curricle? Is it beyond repair, or can we salvage it?"

Devon did not like the look of unease that came over his

co-conspirator's face. The man moved restlessly in his seat, then seemingly unable to find any comfort, he got to his feet. "Come, man, you can tell me straight out. I have not had the contraption long enough to become too attached to it," Devon pressed.

Margate stopped his pacing to face the younger man. "It wasn't an accident that you came to grief. The axle had been sawed through enough for it to break after you were on the road for a while."

Once he had confessed the worst, the old butler waited for his companion to comment. When there was no answer beyond a whistle of surprise from the younger man, Margate's face took on a suspicious look. He lowered himself into the chair once more, his eyes never leaving the other man's face. "I've seen that look on too many corporals' faces when they've been caught pilfering the gin stores. Do I get the feeling that you aren't very surprised that the rig was tampered with?"

Now it was Devon's turn to squirm uncomfortably, only he did not have the luxury of pacing to help formulate his answer. Lord Stanhope had been adamant that he not take any undo risks in ferreting out the guinea smugglers. They were men who disregarded an act of Parliament that forbade the purchase of coinage for more than its value. Three months after the bill was passed, there had been no signs of the trade diminishing; coins were still being purchased in quantity and then presumably shipped out of the country. The revenue men that Devon met in Liverpool and Manchester had tracked down the largest dealer in coins, a cloth merchant named Heaton.

"The general always said I was one of the best men to have at his side, with either one leg or two," Margate stated, drawing himself up into a rigid posture with a mixture of pride and hesitation on his wrinkled face as he waited for Devon's explanation.

"The general certainly knew his men," Devon returned, giving the man a nod of acceptance. "It seems my mission for the government will not be as secretive as I would like it to be."

"Then you didn't come north for the miss," Margate stated.

"No, but let me start at the beginning. I was wounded during the battle, carrying orders from the general to Houston's Seventh Division—a saber cut that glanced off my ribs. You have undoubtedly seen the scar." Devon's hand moved to his side in a reflexive movement. "I was not aware of the loss of the general until days later, but he had asked me to look after his family. I was in hospital for a week, suffering more from fever than my wound, when Old Beaky sent word I was to carry some correspondence to London."

"Most impressive, m'lord," the older man interrupted. For the first time Devon saw a look of approval in the man's eyes and was reluctant to dash his hopes.

"Unfortunately, Wellington was only sending letters, not official despatches. He was not pleased with Fuentes de Onoro, not considering it worth mention or recognition in Parliament, so no one received a promotion or regimental recognition from it," Devon admitted, little realizing his admission did not lower the old servant's opinion of him. "And you'd best leave off that m'lord business. Our young charge has too many fancies of her own without adding a sickly peer to them."

"Just so, Mr. Delane, but what took you such a long time to acknowledge the general's family?" The question held no censure, only curiosity.

"I came down with the fever again once I was home. My family surgeon was able to dose me with enough noxious potions to keep me alive. I contacted my solicitor on a purely routine matter and discovered I had gained a fianceé." He shifted uncomfortably on the bed as any man would who had come so unexpectedly close to the minister's noose. "While I was discussing a possible trip to Dukinfield, Lord Stanhope enlisted my aid in his crusade against the guinea smugglers. He pulled some strings at Whitehall and off I went. I reported to McCrory, the revenue officer at Liverpool, and paid an introductory call to a gentleman named Heaton in Manchester.

Unfortunately, the gentleman was away on business, and McCrory told me to go about my other business."

"But how did you come to be on the road to the lodge? It's nothing more than a local lane."

"I was most kindly mis-directed to it by the innkeeper where I stayed after visiting with Joslyn's aunt and mother," Devon admitted, his scowl telling his companion that he would have further discourse with the person. Then his face cleared as another thought came to mind. "Tell me, Margate, does Lady Amelia ever speak more than a word or two, even when her martinet of a sister is not in residence?"

"Nothing worth the listening, sir. She's a sweet lady and very decorative to have around the house, but there isn't much sense to her, if you pardon my being so blunt," Margate explained with a slightly abashed smile. "The miss ran the household from the time she was old enough; an arrangement that suited everyone. If the truth be known, and it shouldn't leave this room, that's how the general came to buy this place. There really isn't that much hunting in this area, but he needed a bolt hole after a few days at home. He was inordinately fond of his lady, but usually needed a rest from her kind ministrations."

"Yes, I can see his point." After only an hour with Lady Amelia, Devon could understand perfectly the general's point. Lady Amelia must have been the toast of her season; however, looks were not everything in choosing a wife. He was glad to see that Joslyn seemed to take after her father more, even with her fanciful imagination. "Until I can become ambulatory, we shall have to keep close guard against any further help to Mr. Heaton."

"And not discuss it with a certain member of our small brigade. She's liable to turn this place into a fortress waiting for a siege to commence," Margate declared with affectionate malice. He could not remember the last good conversation he had had with another perceptive gentleman. The general and he had spent many a night over a bottle discussing the problem of his ladies. Atkins, who had taken over as butler, was not of a like mind. He was too appreciative of Lady Amelia's kindness in taking him in, and would therefore never utter a word against her. The lady could give him six contradictory instructions in less than an hour, and Atkins still considered her a saint.

"Margate, just how much does Joslyn know about Madame de Stael?" Devon asked, following a new train of thought. From Margate's earlier comments, he was positive that the girl was not a lunatic, just sorely lacking in parts of her education.

"That bloody woman again." Margate gave vent to his feelings on the subject with a few select invectives. "She heard about the Madame after reading that silly book when she was at school. It was about the same time Lady Amelia took her to London to fit the miss for grown-up clothing. Ever since then, that's all she talks about, especially the fact some *tonnish* friend of her mama's treated her poorly for being a military wife."

"Ah, pride and imagination have started wars. There are a few facts our charge needs to learn about her ideal, however," Devon continued with a look of superior male knowledge that mirrored his companion's. "We cannot have such a charming young lady spouting the virtues of a woman who is no better than a respectable courtesan, if there is such a thing."

"Lud, you don't mean—" Margate started, appalled.

"Yes, she is very hospitable when it comes to entertaining gentlemen," Devon confirmed, and gave the older man an angelic smile that erased any of his own activity among the lightskirts. "Fortunately, Joslyn has managed to name her dog based on misinformation as well. Madame is better known by Germaine, rather than Ann-Louise."

"God looks after the innocent and the madman," the old man replied. He gave a sigh of relief that he had been sent an ally in his hour of need after protecting the ladies alone for so long. The excited barking of Ann-Louise from the kitchen brought him back to the matter at hand. "You should get some rest for now. I'll look in later to see if you need any help. We'll try to get you walking as soon as possible, in case we have any unexpected visitors."

"My thoughts exactly. Margate, we have an onerous task

ahead of us," Devon said with a frown. He had little dealings with young women barely out of the nursery and avoided them like the plague whenever possible. Even his three younger sisters were an enigma to him, since he only saw them a few times a year. Joslyn Penderton could be his most wily opponent.

Margate nodded his agreement, barely masking his smile of satisfaction. This buck was just the right man for the young miss. Though he was not aware of it, he was already feeling protective and willing to take some of her education in hand. Margate would see to it that her learning kept well within the bounds of what was proper, but on a loose rein. He was growing to like the idea of Miss Joslyn becoming a marchioness. She had always been a bright child and would quickly learn that she needed a man to guide her through life, and it was to her added advantage that he had position and wealth. The general had known what he was doing when he had given his daughter's care over to Captain Devon Farraday.

"I tell you, Ann-Louise, it just makes no sense. It is not fair," Joslyn muttered as she knelt beside her pet to fasten the leash.

"What isn't fair, young miss?" Margate questioned from the doorway into the kitchen.

"Oh, there you are. You have settled the patient in sufficient comfort, I hope," she returned. Standing upright, she gestured toward the pegs on the wall beside him. "I have unpacked his belongings, and you can attend to whatever it is that will freshen them. Ann-Louise and I are going for a walk."

"Fine, but be sure you don't bring back any more strays. We don't have the bed space, and Mr. Delane won't take kindly to being ignored." The butler gave her a nod of authority; however, there was an uncharacteristic smile on his thin face. "He's taking a bit of a rest now, but remember you promised to entertain him this afternoon."

Joslyn could not bring herself to dignify his ridiculous comment with a reply, knowing she would start ranting at

him if she dared open her mouth. With a firm hand, she lead
Ann-Louise out the kitchen door, not looking back even
when she could swear she heard the sound of laughter
behind her. She could not be sure Margate was laughing,
since the sound was not one she would normally connect
with him.

"What did I tell you, Ann-Louise? Men are the strangest
creatures to be put on this earth," she remarked as they
started down the path that wound around the lodge bound-
aries. "They never make any sense, then complain that
women are confusing."

The animal turned her head and gave her mistress a
sympathetic look before the sound of rustling in the bushes
ahead distracted her. With her ears swinging outward, she
snapped her head forward and began barking furiously.
Joslyn stopped her attempts to run with a firm hand on her
leash.

"You *shtupid* animal, you caused enough trouble yesterday. Mr. Devon was kind enough to take the blame, but I
will not take any more chances." When her pet settled down
to a sedate walk, Joslyn returned to her complaints. "Margate is trying to get me to return home. That must be his
reason for his new mood. Entertain Mr. Delane, indeed.
What did they talk about for so long?"

When Ann-Louise looked up at her in slack-tongued
confusion, Joslyn enlightened her companion. "Just this
morning at breakfast Margate said, 'You'll take the gentleman his meals, then go about your business,'" she repeated
in a perfect mimic of the old man's gravelly tones, "and
now he has granted me permission to entertain Mr. Delane.
There is just no sense to it."

Ann-Louise barked in agreement, attempting to catch her
mistress's attention. Joslyn was standing stock still in the
middle of the path as she again tried to reason out Margate's
change of heart. The spaniel trotted back to nudge Joslyn's
hand in hopes of continuing their walk.

The touch of her pet's wet nose brought Joslyn out of her
reverie. "I'm the fool. Why am I letting this overset me
so?" she asked the world at large with a joyous laugh at her

own stupidity. "I should be overjoyed and take advantage of my good fortune before the old reprobate changes his mind again."

With that, she picked up her skirts and broke into a carefree run, taking her anxious pet by surprise. The two raced down the path as if they had just won their freedom after a long confinement. It was a beautiful day, with the sun shining on the misty hills, and Miss Joslyn Penderton was going to entertain a gentleman this afternoon.

The lodge settled for the night in quiet, comforting sounds, but two of its occupants were wide awake. Devon moved restlessly against the feather mattress that was no longer comfortable after so many hours of forced rest. Just a few short days ago, he had reveled in his freedom after months of convalescence.

Not that his stay at Penderton Lodge would be boring. He smiled as his thoughts drifted back over the events of the day. Miss Joslyn Penderton was certainly not what he had anticipated from the general's fond ramblings of his little girl. Nor was she as he imagined in London after his shock of learning the true state of affairs. Joslyn was an original.

He almost wished he could hide her away from the rest of the world. She was so open and artless as she talked of her preposterous aspirations of taking London by storm. He knew that with only a few weeks among the fashionable she would be turned into the twin of every other simpering debutante, or be shunned and ridiculed as a country bumpkin. Neither would happen, if he had any say in the matter—and he did.

The general had entrusted him with the care of his daughter, and Devon planned to fulfill his obligation. Though he was not ready for the parson's trap, he was positive that his mother or his numerous aunts could be depended upon to find a suitable young man to marry Joslyn. As his bruises healed, Devon would compile a list of necessary traits for her future husband. A unique young lady deserved more than the average man about town.

The objective and challenge of finding the proper husband for Joslyn now gave Devon a real sense of purpose. He closed his eyes and settled down for a restful sleep.

Restful was not how Joslyn felt as she paced around her small chamber in the dead of night. She ignored Ann-Louise's whine to come to bed as she moved silently back and forth. Her head was filled with questions that all centered around Mr. Devon Delane. With his dark eyes and hair, coupled with his intriguing name, he could have stepped out of the pages of the Minerva Press novels her mama was so fond of reading. Joslyn herself only listened out of politeness when Lady Amelia chose to read her favorite passages aloud. Naturally, as a young lady of good sense, Joslyn knew that the stories were romantic balder-dash contrived to make young ladies long for a strong, handsome man to marry who would boss them around, and to her mind, generally make their lives miserable.

"He cannot possibly be a draper," she murmured as she flounced down on her bed, eliciting a whimpered protest from her companion at the end of the bed. "Drapers are thin, dried up little men with a pair of spectacles on the end of their pinched noses."

And why was Margate being so, well, affable? she wondered for almost the hundredth time. Perhaps Devon had run away himself and that was why he was so understanding about her own predicament. He was much too nice—and well muscled—to be a coward, so mayhap his life was in peril. He could be the heir to a great fortune, with a wicked uncle who wanted the money for himself. *Or he could be an ordinary draper,* she thought with disap-pointment as an enormous yawn interrupted her specula-tion.

She lay down and pulled the bedclothes up to her chin, still reluctant to sleep before she reached a conclusion about her injured guest. Turning on her side with her hands tucked under her cheek, she closed her eyes. With a sigh of regret, she wished that Mr. Devon Delane was someone of power and influence. A draper was just not someone who would champion her against the likes of the absent Captain Farraday. If she was ever to get to London and escape the trap of marriage, she needed one of Mama's fierce and arrogant heroes to stand at her side.

As she drifted to sleep, Joslyn imaged Devon outfitted in the armor of one of King Arthur's knights, fighting off a cavalry charge with a bolt of cloth.

4

"JOSLYN, I would think you could allow me to win at least once," Devon complained good-naturedly as his companion rearranged the black and white markers on the inlaid squares of the gaming table beside his bed. They had spent the last two days talking their way through every card game and board game in the lodge. "After all, I am your guest and an invalid. Is there no charity in your gambler's heart?"

Joslyn had beaten him soundly at whist and bouillotte, trounced him at backgammon, and the evening before had taunted him through three games of chess before he admitted defeat. He had hoped a simple game of draughts would allow him to counter her unfathomable stratagems, which he was convinced were based on enthusiastic luck rather than diabolical skill.

His protest was met, as always, with a delightful grin that flashed Joslyn's single and—to his mind—enticingly placed dimple. Her green eyes were sparkling with laughter in the candle glow as she met his sorrowful gaze. "What a pitiful tale, and how shameless of you to try and win on sympathy. Margate says you will be out of bed for good on the morrow. Invalid, indeed."

"Margate, you have come to save a beleaguered, one-armed man from certain doom at the hands of this black-hearted jade," Devon called to the older man who had just entered the room carrying the evening's refreshment—wine for the gentlemen and a pot of chocolate for Joslyn.

"I warned you not to play for money, didn't I? The miss doesn't like to lose," he returned, giving the pair a slight smile, accustomed to their juvenile wrangling by now.

"You never said she always wins," Devon shot back, and reached over to smack Joslyn's hand away when she attempted to begin a new game. "Tut, tut, young woman, have some courtesy, not to mention mercy. Losers go first. See there, Margate, she cheats."

"For that, sir, I am going to leave and take Ann-Louise for her walk. Perhaps some port will put you in a better frame of mind by the time I return," Joslyn announced. She sprang to her feet and called to her pet, who was sleeping peacefully by the fire. "Margate, just leave the cozy on the pot; I shall pour for myself when I return."

As soon as she left the room, Margate hobbled over to place the tray next to Devon's bedside. He took up his position at the window once his hands were free. Neither man spoke until they heard the outside door shut. Devon picked up his glass and relaxed against his bank of pillows as the old servant kept their charge in sight.

"Are you actually going to release me from my confinement to this infernal bed in the morning?"

"Yes, you should start moving around before you stiffen up, now that we know your shoulder is the only damage from your spill and there's been no fever," Margate said, never taking his eyes off the shadowy figures in the yard. "Your other wound hasn't flared up, so it should be safe. We'll keep your arm strapped for a while longer, however, though you can exercise it some when I change the bandage."

"Laying in bed seems to have become my occupation over the last few months," Devon returned, giving a sigh of disgust over his recent ill fortune. "If I am on my feet, I shall have a better chance of running if Joslyn begins her questioning again—though she seems content to beat me all to flinders at games and prattling on about her plans to go to

London. We have now decided that Madame Hyde-Brett would be most suitable for her sobriquet."

"Don't be too complacent over her chatter, my man. Just as she'd said the most outlandish drivel, while playing a game, she goes in for the kill. The more she talks, the more active her mind becomes," the old man warned and reached down for his glass of wine. "She was full of questions during your nap this afternoon. 'Are you truly a cloth merchant? Do you live in the area or London?' I'll be glad when you're ready to travel, and we can stop this masquerade."

"I have been considering that prospect myself. There has been no sign of anyone around the lodge. My accident could simply have been an attempt at robbery, or someone may still be looking for me along the road." Devon stared off into the gloomy shadows of the timbered ceiling over his bed. He studiously avoided meeting his companion's gaze as he prepared to explain his idea. His reasoning was somewhat of a mystery even to himself, and something he did not want to examine too closely at the moment.

There was nothing in his experience that could account for the hollow feeling in the pit of his stomach whenever he thought of leaving Joslyn behind at the hunting lodge. Her fanciful ideas and his lack of activity must have caused his brain to go soft. "We should not leave anything to chance. Joslyn would be safer if she went to stay with my aunt near Stoke-on-Trent. Her relatives will never find her there, and I can join you as soon as my business is finished."

"That's an interesting solution. Do you think this smuggling business will be settled that quickly?" Margate asked.

Devon sensed the other man's sidelong glance, but chose to ignore it while he continued to outline his plans. "I cannot be sure. It would put my mind to rest if she were around more people, somewhere that was not so isolated. There would then be less of a burden on you as well."

"Just how do you plan to convince the miss? You haven't told her tuppence about yourself, and now you suddenly have family in the area." Margate's dry tone grated on Devon's sensitive nerves. The older man remained staring out the window, sipping his wine and throwing off his comments as if discussing the weather.

"My dear sir, that will be the simplest task. It will be a new adventure. Could Joslyn resist the lure of being the guest of a duke's daughter?" Devon answered with more confidence than he actually felt. Joslyn could very well put up a fuss. She did not think like a normal person—or what he considered normal, he amended—so how could he anticipate what she would do?

"And how are you going to explain this duke's daughter?"

Margate was laughing at him, forcing Devon to turn his head to confirm his suspicions. The man stood stiff as a post, however, with a carefully neutral expression on his face. "Well, that is a problem I have not quite solved. I do not think Captain Farraday is ready to make his appearance as yet, so I am open to any suggestions."

"I would be glad to oblige at any other time, but our charge is returning from her evening frolic," the older man remarked, and left his guard post to sit in the chair near the gaming table, ignoring his companion's dark mutterings. Thus far they had kept any suspicious behavior from Joslyn, and Margate hoped they could continue on in that manner. His telling look quieted Devon's heated words.

"Well, my poor-spirited opponent, are you ready to be vanquished yet again by a superior foe?" Joslyn challenged the minute she stepped through the doorway with Ann-Louise prancing around her skirts.

"Overconfidence, my dear, is the sign of an incompetent general," Devon returned. He sat up straighter and gave her his most supercilious look, his left eyebrow ascending to near his ruffled black curls. Her barely smothered grin had him longing for his quizzing glass and a highly starched cravat, the most necessary instruments for a proper set-down. A man just could not obtain the proper respect in a nightshirt.

"What happened to my poor invalid?" Joslyn asked with a slight frown that she hoped Devon would take for concern. His statement was something her father said time and time again, and in an almost identical tone of voice. She immediately thrust the thought aside, since all men sounded the same when they were being pompous.

"He wants revenge."

"He will have to wait until morning. I must be well rested to face such a vengeful opponent." She waved Margate back to his seat when he started to rise, and proceeded to pour her chocolate while waiting for Devon's next sally. Joslyn had not enjoyed herself so much in years as she had in two days of Devon's company. Walking around the bed, she settled herself in the overstuffed armchair near the fire, tucking her feet up under her. When she finished properly draping the skirt of her second-best brown kerseymere, she looked up to find Devon watching her with a very sober expression.

"Oh, dear, what have I done now? Have I imposed too much on your good nature? Mama always scolds me for putting myself forward at the wrong time." Joslyn gave Devon a pleading look of apology, barely pausing to take a breath. "I have presumed too much on our short acquaintance and behaved with unseemly familiarity, I just know it. Devon, no, Mr. Delane, I most humbly beg your pardon, but you see, I have never had any brothers or sisters for companionship, and it has been just like having an older—"

"Joslyn!" Devon raised his voice to the pitch he used only to be heard over cannon fire; however, he did not immediately halt the seemingly endless outpouring.

"—brother," Joslyn finished weakly, struggling to keep her cup and saucer upright from her start of surprise at Devon's shout. Her name was still echoing around the room. She waited with an apprehension that was totally foreign to her nature. Devon was glaring at her, his fierce scowl emphasizing his dark coloring. After a moment his expression softened and allowed her to relax slightly.

"First off, young lady, never apologize to me in that pitiful fashion for something that has not occurred," he instructed in a stern voice that did not encourage interruption. "If anyone is responsible for our rather relaxed manners, I am. The reason I was looking so serious is that

Margate has finally informed me of your reason for being in residence at the lodge. Now, before you raise any objections, I wheedled it out of him. *My* mama has always scolded me for all of my seven-and-twenty years over my insatiable curiosity. I have had hours to ponder why a young lady would be alone in an isolated lodge with only a servant for companionship."

"You think I should return home?" Joslyn asked in a wary tone.

"Certainly not, if you dislike this Captain Farraday so much," Devon was quick to answer. He gave her a gentle smile when her rosy mouth fell open in surprise and her eyes widened in hope. "I have a proposition to put before you as an alternative. My aunt does not live more than a few days' journey from here, and when I tell her of your circumstance, I know she will be more than happy to have you come and stay with her." He raised his hand to prevent Joslyn from rushing into another lengthy speech. "I want you to think this over before giving me an answer. Margate has not given me his approval to travel as yet, so you have some time to mull this over. We shall not speak of it again until you are ready. Agreed?"

Joslyn could only nod. Devon was not going to send her home to face the odious Captain Farraday! He was actually offering to help her in her flight. Perhaps it did not matter that he seemed to be an ordinary draper, or did it mean that he was sympathetic because he was indeed in similar circumstances? She had already made up her mind that his proposition suited her just fine, but kept this to herself since both Devon and Margate would think she was being too impulsive. Neither of them would understand that she was finding the lodge rather dull, with the exception of Devon's company, and a visit to his aunt's would only heighten her adventure, as well as allow her to learn more about Devon's background.

"Well, Miss Penderton, I believe you were boasting at your superiority as a gamester, but were poor-spirited enough to admit I had worn you down," Devon said with a challenging grin.

"Never let it be said that a Penderton cried craven," she returned, giving him a grin of her own that clearly stated she would win, tired or not.

"Then shall we proceed?" Devon bolstered himself up on his pillows to show he was up to her skill. He was heartened to see that her good humor had returned, and hoped he would never see that chastened expression on her lovely face again. It had wounded him almost as much as her admission that she looked upon him as an older brother. He did not have time to examine either thought, however, since he needed to focus all his attention on the game before him. He barely had time to register Margate's nod of approval from where he stood behind Joslyn before the lady answered his opening move.

"Devon, is it enjoyable being a man?"

Joslyn's question took him by surprise as he lay with his good arm tucked behind his head, staring up at the canopy of trees over their heads. He had been allowed out of bed for a day and a half, willingly acceding to any plan of Joslyn's that took him out of doors. Today they had packed a picnic, while Margate paid a visit to the Penderton home.

Joslyn made a pretty picture, dressed in a green-spotted sprig muslin walking gown, with her legs tucked under her where she sat next to him on the quilt. The remains of their repast were littered around them. The afternoon had been occupied with aimless ambling not far from the lodge, Ann-Louise flushing out every four-legged animal in the vicinity, and after partaking of a cold lunch, Joslyn reading from a book that Devon had found at the bottom of his valise. A friend had recommended *Sense and Sensibility* before he left London, but only now did Devon appreciate the irony of his selection as the least sensible person he knew read to him from the amusing tale.

"What did you say?" He suddenly realized that her question was her own, not one posed by the characters in the novel.

"I wanted to know if it is enjoyable being a man," she repeated, closing the maroon leather-bound book and resting it in her lap. The breeze was ruffling her curls, which she did not notice while giving him a solemn look.

"You are suddenly very pensive, my dear," Devon responded.

"I have been considering your invitation to your aunt's home and thinking how none of this would have been the least bit necessary if I were a man," she said with a sigh that suggested something between disgust and resignation. "Papa would not have found the need to burden me with this Captain Farraday, instead he would have bought my colors and had me in his brigade, fighting at his side. I could have chosen who I wanted to marry, if I chose to marry at all, just as you have not married."

"Do you really imagine this Farraday person is the devil incarnate? Would marriage truly be such a horrible affair?" Devon made sure his tone was not in any way as anxious as his feelings on the matter. He carefully remained in his lounging position, idly twirling a blade of grass between his fingers.

"Oh, I suppose he really is not a monster. After all, Papa would have only wanted the best for me; however, he is a military man," Joslyn answered, giving a careless shrug as if that should be explanation enough.

"And what has that to say about the matter?"

"I suppose you have not had much acquaintance with the military set. They are accustomed to having their own way, expecting orders to be obeyed without the least question," she informed him as if explaining the facts to a child. "Actually, now that I consider it, Papa was a typical man, only more so. He looked on Mama and me as an extension of his brigade, though he tempered his orders with hugs and kisses, along with an occasional present."

"Yes, I can see your point." Devon had great difficulty in maintaining his composure. The general had been a stern but fair taskmaster, who had never softened toward his men in any circumstance. Sir Quentin certainly had never displayed a softer side to his personality when on duty.

"You cannot say you would like having a bride chosen

for you without your consent or be told when you should marry," Joslyn added.

Devon considered her questions, wondering how she would react to knowing that she was his chosen bride, selected without his consent. Being a man had not made one whit of difference. He could understand Joslyn's desire to have a choice, but she did not comprehend that she was not knowledgeable enough in the ways of the world to lead her life in London as planned. He made a pledge to himself, and Joslyn, that he would seek her opinions on the young gentlemen who would be suitable as her husband. He would never force her to marry a man she could not like, nor would he coerce his young sisters when their time came.

"No, I would like to marry the lady of my choice, but so far I have not found a single lady who would be a suitable life companion," he stated with certainty, then remembered his role as Mr. Delane, the draper. "Actually, I have little enough to offer at the moment, but when I am able to purchase my own establishment, I shall seriously consider the matter."

"You see, it is a simple matter for you. You make your way in the world and decide when it is time for you to marry," Joslyn remarked, wrinkling her nose at him to show her displeasure.

"I wonder how Margate is faring on his errand?" Devon felt the need to change the subject with all possible haste, and to forget the sudden desire he felt to kiss the six tantalizing freckles that dusted Joslyn's delightfully turned-up nose.

"I can vouchsafe that he and Atkins are spending a good portion of this day cataloguing my numerous sins. That is their favorite way of passing the time, whether I am present or not."

"Yes, Atkins, my friend, we'll be having a wedding soon enough, mark my words," Margate stated with real satisfaction as he bit into one of Mrs. Ferris's apple tarts—his third. "It won't be that spotty Gervais, but a peer of the realm."

"Her ladyship is having the vapors every hour over where her little darling could be, and all ya do is boast of fancy nobs and stuff yer face," returned his companion, who helped himself to his fourth tart without a thought to his ample waist.

"She hasn't a need to worry. We'll be off to the marquess' aunt in Stoke-on-Trent until he finishes his business, then he'll be taking care of the young miss," Margate continued. He ignored Atkins' remarks about Lady Amelia, who sometimes had sinking spells over the prospect of rain on a day she chose to go out in the carriage.

"Yer sure this cove means ta marry the miss, then?"

"Positively. The pair of them are smelling of April and May without even being aware of it."

"Then you'd best be startin' the journey on the morrow," Mrs. Ferris put in, setting down the tray she had retrieved from the sitting room only moments before returning to the kitchen. "That little toad Gervais has been given his orders from that mother of his. He's to start looking for the miss in the morning."

"And I suppose he thought of the lodge as the most likely place to start?" Margate asked the question, knowing full well what had undoubtedly taken place.

"Lady Amelia was natterin' away about what was to be done about the general's possessions, and what was she goin' to do with a huntin' lodge," Mrs. Ferris admitted with a look of defeat. "Naturally, that sister of hers took it into her head that that's where the miss has gone to ground."

Margate got to his feet as fast as his wooden leg would allow. "I'd best be on my way. It's a good thing that His Lordship lent me his horse for the trip. Old Cornwallis wouldn't have been up to the speed I'll need on my return journey. Not a word to anyone that I've been here, or where the miss has gone, especially to Lady Amelia."

Atkins would have protested the slight to his mistress, but the older man was already on his way out the door with Mrs. Ferris on his heels carrying the basket of provisions he forgot in his haste to leave. The disgruntled butler would have followed the pair had the sitting room bell not sounded a summons for his presence. He levered himself up with his single arm and went to see how he could best serve Lady Amelia.

"You will not take off that bandage until Margate says you may, Devon," Joslyn protested as they came in sight of the lodge.

"But, Joslyn, it is a dashed nuisance, and it itches," Devon returned with heat. "I could not even get up off the quilt without assistance."

"I did not mind in the least—Ann-Louise, will you please settle down? I shall let you off your leash in just a moment," Joslyn scolded as the dog started barking furiously and straining at her leash. Joslyn had trouble maintaining her one-handed grip, carrying the picnic hamper in her other hand, when the dog lunged forward at the end of the leather strap. "What has gotten into you, you *shtupid* animal?"

"I think I hear someone coming," Devon announced, cocking his head to the side to concentrate on the sound of approaching hoofbeats. He relaxed his guard, letting his hand fall to his side away from the pistol concealed under his shirt when Margate came into view. "Ah, Margate. I had not expected him back before nightfall."

"Ann-Louise!" Joslyn called after her pet, who had taken advantage of one moment's distraction and pulled her leash from her mistress's grasp. She did not run toward the horse and cart as expected, however, but shot toward the stand of trees near the stable. There was a rustling in the undergrowth as soon as the dog disappeared from sight. Her increased growling and barking could be heard and then, to the surprise of Joslyn and Devon who had started after her, the sound of a man cursing.

Moments later a surprising tableau came bursting out of the trees. A blond-haired man was grappling with Ann-Louise, who had attached her teeth and jaws to the back of his leg and would not let go. Joslyn cried out in alarm and would have run to the dog's assistance if Devon had not thrown his arm around her shoulders. She dropped the wicker picnic basket as she struggled briefly until his grunt of pain made her realize she had struck his bandaged arm.

A movement from her right distracted her from Devon's momentary distress. Margate had pulled the cart up at the edge of the yard and clambered down. He was approaching Ann-Louise and the intruder in his hobbling semblance of a run. "Devon, you must do something. The man has a knife," Joslyn cried.

Devon was torn between protecting Joslyn and going to the old man's rescue. "Joslyn, I want your solemn promise that you will stand here and do nothing to put yourself in danger."

"I shall not get in the way," she promised, her eyes never leaving the trio across the yard. The intruder had managed to thrust Ann-Louise aside momentarily, turning all his attention toward Margate. The older man armed himself with a shovel that was leaning against the side of the stable. In an agile move, he swung it upward, just as Ann-Louise renewed her attack.

Margate was able to catch the man's knife hand with the blade of the shovel, sending the wicked-looking implement sailing into the trees. Unfortunately, the man did not want to surrender. Instead he snarled like a cornered animal and hurled himself at his assailant. Joslyn heard Devon give vent to a heated oath before he ran toward the two men. She did not hesitate for a moment, and ran for the lodge with one purpose in mind. Margate's Baker rifle was always kept loaded just inside the door.

She grabbed the rifle from its resting place without giving any thought to its weight, though she remembered her father's instructions. She carried the weapon firmly under one arm with the barrel resting on her forearm, and did not cock it before she was ready to fire. The three men did not appear to have moved in her absence. Margate was still fighting for control of the shovel with the intruder. Both Devon and Ann-Louise were dancing around the combatants, his shouts being drowned out by her barking—at any other time, Joslyn would have found this scene very entertaining. The seriousness of the situation was clearly demonstrated, however, by the pistol in Devon's hand.

While he tried to maneuver around the men, Margate kept getting between him and the intruder.

Joslyn walked calmly with carefully placed footsteps to where the picnic hamper had fallen, the exact spot where Devon had instructed her to stay. With a real sense of purpose, she raised the rifle and took careful aim, adjusting her stance to accommodate the weight of the weapon to her slender stature. Sucking in her breath, she cocked the rifle with a slow, even movement, closed her eyes, and squeezed the trigger.

All sounds of the men's struggle ceased at the report of the rifle. There was only the reverberation of the gunshot echoing through the clearing, accompanied by the startled cries of birds in the neighboring trees. Joslyn opened one eye to see if the shot had had the desired effect, then opened the other, allowing a satisfied smile to spread over her face.

The shot had drawn the combatants apart. The three men stood frozen in place. Devon, the first to recover, raised his pistol and aimed it point blank at the blond-haired man. Margate and the stranger still held the shovel between them, each gripping it with both hands.

"Now, sir, release the shovel and step back," Devon instructed. Ann-Louise seemed to find the sudden lack of activity disagreeable and was ready for more sport. She scampered around Devon's feet, barking her disapproval.

"Joslyn, call off this idiot dog of yours," Devon called out at the same moment the frisky animal jumped up and knocked against his leg.

That was all the intruder needed. He twisted the shovel and pushed his opponent backward, all in one quick movement. Margate cried out in pain and fell against Devon. Both men tumbled to the ground, with Devon attempting to hold his cocked pistol out of harm's way. The stranger turned and fled into the trees.

Joslyn tossed the rifle aside, quickly forgetting in her distress all her papa's instructions on the handling of firearms. With her skirts pulled high, she ran to the two men who were attempting to untangle themselves with little success. Their efforts were greatly hampered by Margate's wooden leg and Devon's strapped arm.

"My God, did she shoot you?" Devon gasped, still winded from the impact of the older man's body.

His words stopped Joslyn just as she was about to kneel on the ground and offer her assistance. Margate struggled to a sitting position, cradling his right hand against his chest.

"No, it's my wrist," he reported, his face contorted in pain as he looked up at Joslyn's indignant figure. She stood with her hands on her hips, glaring at the two dusty men on the ground with Ann-Louise sniffling curiously around them.

"Well, miss, are you just going to stand there?" the old man grumbled, looking from her to Devon, who still lay on his back in the dirt. He knew what had caused her angry look. The younger man was oblivious to the female rage about to break over his head, and his present discomfort was increased as Ann-Louise began licking Devon's face.

"Ann-Louise, stop that," Joslyn ordered and grabbed at the dog's leash. "His face is filthy."

"*I* am filthy?" Devon sputtered as he attempted to sit up by rocking his upper body until he could find a handhold with his right hand and prop himself upright. "And what got me filthy, Miss Penderton? Your wild shooting, when you gave me your solemn promise to stay still, and that half-wit dog of yours."

"Wild shooting? I shot over your heads, so the only thing I may have hit was a bird. Let me tell you, Mr. Delane, I learned to shoot when I was a mere child," Joslyn returned, unable to resist the urge to stamp her foot to emphasize her point before she walked around him with exaggerated care. She picked up the shovel from where it had fallen, then used it to help Margate stand. When that was accomplished, she returned her attention to Devon. "And I did not promise to stay still. I said I would not get in the way."

"You could have injured one of us just the same," he asserted. He was unwilling to give up the argument which was clearly indicated by the jut of his chin.

"In case anyone is interested, I don't believe my wrist is

broken, just sprained," Margate interpolated. Both the young people had the good sense to look ashamed of themselves for forgetting his injury. "At another time we can discuss the miss's prowess with a rifle—which I had a hand in, I might add—though she's never cared for firearms. For now, miss, you help up Mr. Delane, dirt and all. You can wash up before you wrap my wrist. We have more important things to worry about with your spotty cousin coming to pay us a call on the morrow."

He walked toward the lodge using the shovel as a staff to aid his balance. Joslyn did his bidding, but not before she carefully picked up Devon's pistol and uncocked it. She did not have time to consider where the gun had materialized from as she worried over Margate's statement. It was fortunate she had already decided to accept Devon's invitation to visit his aunt, even though it was possible he might recant after her childish tantrum.

Neither of them spoke as they followed Margate to the lodge. Devon's face was a thundercloud that kept her from voicing even a halfhearted apology.

"But why should I not wear men's clothing as a disguise? Some of Devon's clothes would not be too large," Joslyn demanded a few hours later. Joslyn, Devon, and Margate were discussing their departure the next day while dining on some of the plunder from Mrs. Ferris's basket. "Gervais will be looking for an old man and a girl. What could be more brilliant than traveling as two gentlemen and a servant?"

"Joslyn, my dear, I doubt that any disguise would ever fool anyone into believing you were anything but female," Devon answered, sharing a look of affectionate exasperation with Margate.

Joslyn had been arguing for her masculine costume, with little success, for ten minutes past. She had only managed to amuse Devon. His usual good humor had returned when Margate informed him he could wear his arm in a sling since the older man's own injury would keep him from strapping Devon's arm properly, and there was no question

of Joslyn doing the task. The new bandage caused the
young lady to liken the two men to bookends, one with his
right arm in a sling and one with his left arm the same.

"But, Devon—"

"It is not even worth considering," he interrupted. He set
down his fork, knowing his capon would have to wait until
the matter was settled. "You may be slender, but the curves
of your figure would give you away, and then where would
we be? You may consider your cousin a fool; however,
there are other people we shall encounter. When Gervais
starts talking of a young female who has gone missing, the
first thing that will come to mind is two men traveling with
an oddly shaped boy."

"I am not oddly shaped," she stated with an indignant
flounce in her chair. "There is nothing wrong with my
figure."

"Precisely, for a young woman. In fact, I would say it's
quite exceptional, but not as a boy." Devon gave Joslyn an
intent look to help make his point. He could barely repress
a grin of satisfaction as the import of his words finally sank
into Joslyn's overly active mind.

She blinked at him like a baby owl, then did not seem to
know where to look as she blushed. With one last peek
across the table at Devon from beneath her long lashes, she
subsided with a barely audible, "Oh."

Devon realized he had just discovered a valuable weapon
for settling an argument with the now embarrassed young
lady. Flattery seemed foreign to her. Perhaps she was not far
different from others of her species, whose vanity was
easily flattered, though Joslyn's blushes were much more
appealing than the knowing smiles and speculative glint in
the eyes of other fair damsels. Margate's stern face and
raised eyebrows reminded him that Joslyn was much more
impressionable than any other young lady of his acquaintance. He would have to be careful in his compliments,
using them judiciously, to avoid Joslyn developing an
untimely tendre for him before he could locate a suitable
young man for her. It just would not do.

"We do have another problem, sir." Margate's words

kept Devon from dwelling on the sinking feeling that overcame him at the thought of an eligible connection for Joslyn. "Thanks to our sneak thief, neither of us is fit to drive the horses, even if we used my Cornwallis. We shall have to entrust our safety on the road to the miss, I suppose. Perhaps waiting here for Gervais wouldn't be such a poor plan after all."

"Margate," Joslyn exclaimed. She stopped fidgeting with her utensils to glare at the old man. "I might not be able to handle a fancy rig like Devon's, but I have driven your cart countless times."

"I was just testing you, miss. You had grown so quiet." The old man quirked up the ends of his lips in the closest he ever came to a smile.

"Men are the most horrible creatures on the earth," Joslyn declared in return before standing up and calling to Ann-Louise. "We ladies shall retire for the evening, so you can continue talking about me behind my back at great length. I need to rest for our journey. I am sure with your superior intellect you can figure out how to clear away the dishes with your unencumbered hands."

She retained her rigid pose as she walked across the great room. Ann-Louise sensed her mistress' mood and followed suit by prancing close to her side. Once the young lady was behind the closed door of her room, however, she gave into the excited laughter that began bubbling up inside her at Margate's admission she would have to drive. That almost made up for being unable to wear a disguise. Men truly did not have an aptitude for adventure, it was clear to see; but allowing her to drive was a small step in the right direction.

As she went through her nightly ritual, Joslyn found her eyes drawn more than once to the small mirror on her dresser. Once she combed her hair the required strokes, she gave in to temptation. Dressed only in her nightgown, she twisted and turned in front of the mirror, occasionally pulling the material taut at her hips, her waist, and finally her breasts. The last caused her to sigh in defeat.

Devon could not have meant what he said about her curves. Her waist was small, and her hips were not terribly bad, but she had nothing above the waist to recommend her, especially to a gentleman who traveled the country. With one last look in the mirror, she shuffled back to her bed, snuggling under the bedclothes with Ann-Louise. In spite of her disappointing discovery about her figure, her blood was singing with excitement.

Tomorrow Devon was leaving, but she was going with him on a brand new adventure. After a brief stop in Manchester, they were going to his aunt's house. Neither Gervais nor Captain Farraday would have a single clue to her whereabouts. As she drifted off to sleep, Joslyn thought it really was a shame that Devon was only a draper.

5

"Yes, Devon, I *see* the wagon, some two miles down the road," Joslyn acknowledged, resisting the impulse to scream in frustration. After three hours on the road, she was having trouble remembering that he meant well in his instructions. At the speed Devon insisted on maintaining, they would not reach Manchester for another sennight. Perhaps she should ask if he would like her to get out and lead his precious horse the rest of the way, or even hitch her to the cart instead.

"Just keep a steady hand, miss, like I taught you," Margate interpolated, none too soon. Joslyn was about to remind Devon she had yet to overturn a vehicle or come to harm, unlike some people she was too polite to mention.

"I have not had a chance to break in this team yet. I am not certain how either will respond in a single hitch," Devon stated, seemingly unaware that this bit of news had been announced at ten-minute intervals since they began their journey. This was something he had not worried about the previous day when he willingly lent his horse to Margate. Neither horse seemed to notice the change in drivers. One of Devon's chestnuts was in harness and the other hitched behind, walking placidly next to Cornwallis.

"Margate, are you sure Gervais will not suspect we were staying at the lodge?" Joslyn asked in desperation. She was grasping at any thread of conversation that would take

Devon's mind off his horses. Though why she was bothering to worry, she could not comprehend. Gervais would undoubtedly pass them on the road soon.

"We left it almost as we found it, except for the dust," the old man returned. "Your cousin hasn't the brain power to notice the lack of dust, and I didn't muck out the stable this morning for good measure." He paused as the wagon passed them with a safe distance between the two vehicles, but kicking up a small cloud of dust. "Now that the road is clear, you might put on a little speed. It's possible he won't linger at the lodge, and I don't fancy meeting him on the open road if he comes this way."

Though she managed to bite back a triumphant exclamation at the request for speed, Joslyn could not resist a sidelong glance at Devon. She regretted the lapse almost immediately, her hands unconsciously loosening on the reins. The young chestnut noticed the change of tension at once and picked up his pace, jerking his passengers in the process. Joslyn recovered control quickly, but her cheeks grew warm at Margate's abrupt cough from behind her. Knowing all too well from past experience that the sound was suppressed laughter, she did not dare look at Devon to see his reaction.

She decided her best option was silence, and the others seemed to agree. The miles went by more easily without Devon's constant instructions. Joslyn began to relax and enjoy her adventure again. Her wandering thoughts lead to Devon's aunt. Would the lady be *sympatico* to a runaway girl she had never met? Could she truly count on either Devon or his aunt to help extricate her from this horrible engagement to Captain Farraday?

Just the thought of Farraday made her angry. He had turned her life upside down, but he could not bring himself to make an appearance. Surely a gentleman, one hand-picked by her father, would have better manners, she told herself for the hundredth time. She knew she was not a prize on the marriage market—her aunt had explained that to her often enough—but she was passable, certainly good enough for a mere captain. Even Devon seemed to enjoy her company.

"Now, miss, where have your tortuous thoughts taken you this time?" Margate's question was accompanied by a whine from Ann-Louise and brought Joslyn out of her brown study.

"I was just wondering what Manchester will be like. I think Papa took me there once as a child, but I do not remember the trip," she returned, dismissing the *shtupid* captain from her mind. Another more appealing thought took its place. "Is Papa's solicitor in Manchester?"

"Could be. I don't recollect, but we have more pressing matters to consider," Margate answered. "This mongrel of yours had been pestering me to be let loose for the last mile, and my stomach tells me that it's near lunch time."

"There is a lane just ahead, off to the right, that leads into a nice stand of trees," Devon put in, watching Joslyn's profile with interest. He was beginning to know when she was plotting something, and the tilt of her chin told him that he and Margate needed to be on their toes. The lady was up to something.

Exactly what she was plotting he could not fathom, but he was sure that it did not bode well for him. His exaggerated worries over his horses had put her out of sorts; however, it had kept her from asking any searching questions. Joslyn had yet to wonder why some ruffian had been lurking in the woods near the lodge. Though Margate thought she would dismiss the incident as a random thief, Devon did not think they would be so lucky. While the lady practiced some topsy-turvy logic, she was intelligent and prone to pounce on the one item of information that was the most dangerous.

"Devon, are you sure your aunt will not mind having an unexpected guest?" Joslyn asked some twenty minutes later. She sat alternately munching on a crust of bread and a slice of cheese from the lunch basket. Margate was tending to the horses and muttering dark imprecations at Ann-Louise, who was tethered to the wheel of the cart.

"Aunt Joan adores guests. She's always complaining that no one ever comes to visit her anymore, that my mother and sisters are much too busy—" he broke off, suddenly realizing the trap that he had stepped into without any warning. Damn Joslyn and her expressive, innocent face. He could see her delight in his unconscious mention of his family. Devon found he was intrigued by the emerald sparkle of her eyes before he had a chance to collect his thoughts.

"You have sisters? How many do you have? How old are they? Do they live near your aunt?" She managed the questions all in one rush of breath, sitting up eagerly from her reclining position against a tree.

"Three sisters. Eileen is seventeen, Judith is fifteen, and Barbara is— Barbara is twelve," he managed. If he started with the bare facts, perhaps he could think of a believable explanation why his sisters lived in Yorkshire and he was plying his trade in Manchester and not York. He could not say his mother was already immersed in planning for Eileen's London debut next spring. Perhaps by staying close to the truth he might be able to salvage the situation. "My family is originally from the east, but I came to this area to make my fortune. Aunt Joan has no children, so her husband agreed to help establish me in a trade. Unfortunately, he died just as I was finishing my apprenticeship."

"Oh, dear, that must have been terrible for your aunt. No children and no husband," Joslyn said in sympathy. The mournful look in her eyes almost had Devon confess that his uncle was hale and hearty, making life miserable for some poor undersecretary at Whitehall. "Perhaps we should go straight to your aunt's house instead of taking a side trip to Manchester first."

"That would be the easiest route, but I have to report to my employer as soon as possible. I am already long overdue and could get the sack if he thought I was not reliable," Devon stated quickly, perhaps too quickly from the sudden narrowing of Joslyn's gaze. The sound of Margate approaching from behind allowed him to give an inward sigh of relief. Any interruption was welcome. He could not be

sure that Joslyn believed a word he said. Bustling about to
clear the remains of lunch and preparing to travel would
distract her temporarily and give him time to think of more
lies.

He is keeping something from me, Joslyn decided as
Devon gave her a hand up onto the seat of the cart. He
refused to meet her curious glance and only mumbled in
response to her thanks. He had suddenly looked discom-
forted the moment she mentioned Manchester. Was she
right after all? Devon was not a draper, or was he? Her
elation was short-lived as she considered the most likely
reason for his deception. Did he have a sweetheart in
Manchester?

She preferred to think he was masquerading as a draper
for a noble purpose, not chasing after some simpering miss.
She could not think what the purpose could possibly be,
however. It needed serious consideration, she decided, and
set her mind to the task, ignoring the murmur of the men's
voices behind her. Devon could have lost his inheritance at
the gambling tables and left home to reclaim it. But why
would he have come west? His sister might have been
dishonored by some scoundrel, and Devon was set on
revenge. That could not be right either, since Devon had not
seemed worried when he mentioned his sisters.

Joslyn wished that she had paid closer attention when her
mother read her novels aloud. Her quiet village life had not
prepared her to speculate on the trials and tribulations of the
outside world. She would simply have to redouble her
efforts to determine Devon's purpose.

"Devon, why do you want to stop here? We have barely
reached the outskirts of the city," Joslyn protested at his
instruction to pull into the yard of the Bonnie Prince Inn.
The outline of smokestacks and buildings sat beguilingly on
the horizon, cunningly made more attractive by a slight
haze. "It seems to me that we should be staying at a
crowded inn that is hidden in the heart of the city if we want
to avoid Gervais."

"Gervais isn't going to be looking for you in Manchester

so soon. Once he finds the lodge deserted, he'll have to return home to that harping mother of his for further instructions," Margate returned in a dampening tone that told her not to argue. He did not seem to mind that he was contradicting his own words from earlier in the day.

She pretended the older man had not spoken since she was more interested in how Devon would explain the matter. "This is not a wise choice, Devon," she continued. "You said that he would be asking for a girl traveling with a servant, and here we are in plain sight."

"This is where we are going to spend the night, young lady. I know that it is clean and, more importantly, within my budget." He jumped down lightly from the cart, his balance unimpaired by his sling, and stood glaring up at her. Placing his free hand on his hip and tapping one foot, he waited for her agreement. He made an imposing figure in his brown riding coat and tan breeches above his glossy boots.

When she did not reply, he continued in a low voice meant only for her ears. "Next time you run away, make sure you find a bloke with plenty of the ready. This time you have to make due with a junior draper who has to save his blunt."

"Oh." Joslyn could not think of anything else to say, almost ashamed of her persistence. Poor Devon did not like admitting that he could not afford better accommodations, and foolishly she had had to force the issue. Suitably chastened, she climbed down and took Ann-Louise's leash without another word. She took her bandbox from Margate and accepted Devon's arm up the stone steps into the inn.

"Greetings, Your Lordship, will ya be stoppin' at the Bonnie Prince?" said a rotund, ruddy faced man as he stepped into the entryway from the noisy public room behind him. Though his smile was affable when he spoke to Devon, the man eyed Joslyn's faded sprig muslin and her bare head with a discerning eye.

"I would like two rooms for the night, one for my—my sister and another for myself and my manservant," Devon stated easily as if he was used to issuing orders to toadying individuals, ignoring Joslyn's slight choking behind her hand. He also did not bother to correct the innkeeper's misconception that he was a member of the peerage. Undoubtedly the service would not be as good for a common draper, though there was something in the way Devon carried himself that suggested quality.

"No problems a'tall, m'lord, Herbert Gantry is pleased ta serve ya. If you'll jest step over to the desk here, we'll arrange the matter." Gantry wiped his hands on his apron, then made a wide sweep with his right arm for Devon and his companion to proceed him. "I'll have my nephew fetch your baggage upstairs. Just set it down there."

"Dulcie, Tully, where have ya got to? I need ya," the little man bellowed from behind Joslyn, causing her to jump and nearly step on Ann-Louise while she placed her bandbox next to Devon's satchel. Gantry gave her a benign smile that showed a gap between his front teeth. "Nice little doggy, Your Ladyship."

Joslyn knew that the man would have had Ann-Louise out in the yard if Devon had not been present. A trampling of feet from two sides interrupted her less than charitable thoughts. The first person to arrive was a plump, blond girl with rosy cheeks and a friendly smile—especially at the sight of Devon—who was only a few years younger than Joslyn. The boy, Tully, was only a few steps behind, coming in from the yard.

Ann-Louise yapped a friendly greeting at the new arrivals, causing Tully to move closer to the girl, who had to be his older sister from the resemblance. As he eyed the dog warily, Joslyn took pity on him, giving him an encouraging smile. "Would you like to pet her? She is really very friendly. In fact, she will want to shake your hand. Say hello to Tully, Ann-Louise."

The spaniel immediately sat up on her haunches and prettily offered her right paw to the boy. Tully hesitated for a moment before squaring his thin shoulders and taking a step forward. In spite of the rigid set of his body, as if ready to run at any sudden move from the animal, he reached out and briefly touched Ann-Louise's paw. When he was done, he stepped back at a safe distance, giving Joslyn a toothless smile of triumph.

"Here boy, no more of this folderol. Ya takes His Lordship and Ladyship's bags up ta the rooms at the back of the house," Gantry snapped at his nephew, but was beaming again when he turned to Devon. "They be our best rooms away from the yard, so ya won't be bothered by the noise and the dust. Be there anythin' else, m'lord?"

"Yes, my good man, a private parlor for our meals. My sister is very delicate," he confided, seeming to puff out his chest further with each word, looking down his nose at the portly innkeeper. "She is also a little spoiled and must take her puppy with her everywhere."

"Oh, Devon, you are so good to me," Joslyn purred, unable to resist joining his playacting. If he was going to be some toplofty nob, she could certainly act the part of his wayward sibling. She batted her eyelashes at him for good measure and was rewarded by a severe frown. A commotion to her right kept Devon from scolding her.

"Oh, dear." Joslyn was hard pressed not to laugh at the sight of poor Tully sprawled on the floor. He seemed to have tripped over her bandbox, and Ann-Louise thought it was a new game. She pounced on the boy, licking his face to show her approval.

"Ann-Louise," Devon ordered before Joslyn could speak, and took the leash from her. He turned to Gantry with a speaking look at his "sister" and her pet. "I must apologize, Mr. Gantry. My sister has yet to teach this beast any manners. I hope the boy was not harmed."

Gantry was at a loss for words, his face turning an interesting shade of red. Finally he managed, "No problem, m'lord. Tully, take the bags abovestairs."

With a regal nod, Devon took Joslyn's arm to lead her to the stairway. At the bottom of the stairs he handed her Ann-Louise's leash. Joslyn was about to reprimand his high-handed manner when he bent forward and kissed her on the cheek.

"Not a word, sister dear," he said in a low voice. "The man probably would have beaten the boy for his clumsiness, and that would have been unjust. Tully was so preoccupied by gazing at you in rapt admiration that he walked into the baggage. Now go up to your room and freshen up for dinner. You cannot disappoint Tully, can you?"

Joslyn quickly swallowed her words, her hand unconsciously going to her cheek and capturing the fleeting warmth of his lips. Suddenly shy of the amusement in Devon's brown eyes, she lowered her lashes before bobbing a quick curtsy. "As you wish, brother dear."

"I shall see what is keeping Margate and be up directly to check our accommodations." Devon watched her ascent, wishing that the young lady was always so easily led.

An hour later over dinner, Joslyn could not hold her peace a minute longer. "Devon, surely having a private parlor is an extravagance. I would not have minded eating in the public room. After all, you had to pay for two rooms as well."

"Joslyn, we are not in such dire straits as that. I do not think you would have found the public room so enjoyable. I certainly would not have had a peaceful dinner," Devon returned with easy good humor. The meal and the quiet room seemed to have a relaxing effect, diminishing his irritable manner from earlier in the day. Of course, Gantry's way of treating him like visiting royalty could be the cause.

"Why is that?" Joslyn asked immediately, then made a clicking noise with her tongue. "Will you stop sneaking food to Ann-Louise? She will become positively roly-poly."

"I simply cannot resist such a lovely pair of brown eyes," Devon said. *Or green ones, for that matter*, he finished silently, then dismissed the thought with a sense of unease. "I shall try to do better. And the reason I would not have a quiet meal in the public room is because of a certain young lady. She would be constantly pointing out every new individual, speculating on his business, real or imagined. In turn, every gentleman in the room would be too curious about this inquisitive young lady. Perhaps another one would offer to do some small service for you."

"Tully only carried my bandbox up to my room and asked if I needed my shoes shined." Joslyn knew she was blushing and could not understand the reason for it. It certainly was not the indulgently amused look he directed at her.

"His voice broke three times, and he tripped over Ann-Louise's leash twice as he left your room because he was gazing at you so worshipfully," Devon said firmly, his slight smile broadening to an outright grin. "If I had known that you were going to start collecting gallants so easily along the way, I would have thought twice about offering my services."

"Devon, be serious. He was only being helpful," she returned with a note of censure in her voice. She could not help being pleased, however, that Devon thought Tully had admired her, though the stripling was barely past fourteen years of age. If the boy had been a few years older—a likely candidate for a knight errant—she might have had some hope in telling Captain Farraday to go about his business, if she ever saw the man. "Now, tell me what sights we shall see tomorrow."

Her question was greeted by a long silence. Devon was very interested in the partridge he was awkwardly dissecting with one hand encumbered by his sling, frowning at the bird with great concentration. Joslyn did not offer her assistance as she had to Margate earlier. As the silence lengthened, she looked to the older man for a possible explanation. He looked up, and catching her eyes trained on him, cleared his throat.

"Don't pester the man so when he's trying to digest his food, miss." Margate deigned to put down his fork for the first time since the meal began and took an exaggerated amount of time wiping his mouth with his napkin. "You always want to know what's going to happen on the morrow two days ahead of time."

"I am not pestering you, am I, Devon? I simply like to anticipate what is ahead so I can enjoy every minute."

"What you shall see tomorrow will be the inn and the yard outside."

She could not believe what he said at first. Looking from

one man to the other, a sinking feeling overtook her, making her lose her appetite. Devon and Margate were watching her with identical expressions—grim determination. With a feeling of dread, she asked the question that was trembling on her lips. "Surely you jest?"

"No, I am very serious. You will stay at the inn tomorrow while I take care of my business." Devon snuck another tidbit to Ann-Louise, but Joslyn was too angry to care at the moment.

"That is ridiculous. How can you even consider making me stay here?" She knew her voice was becoming shrill, something she hated in her Aunt Verity, but she could not believe what was happening. Her splendid adventure was falling apart before her eyes once more.

"I have business to attend to tomorrow, young lady, so I cannot act as a tour guide to an inquisitive child." Devon's voice was harsh, and all the humor had gone from his expression as he watched her mutinous face. "You cannot think that Margate will hobble around at your side, or worse, allow you to scamper around the town with no more escort than Ann-Louise? There are times when you think only of your pleasure, not about the reality of the situation. If you want to live in London, Joslyn, you are going to have to become much more thoughtful and responsible. A lady is judged by how she behaves."

Blinking back hot tears of resentment at his unexpected attack, Joslyn had to wait for a moment to respond. She did not want her voice to quiver as she defended herself. Devon was being so unfair and presumptuous to lecture her, as if she was an idiotic child. "I am so sorry I spoke before I thought. Of course, you have your livelihood to consider, and since you are familiar with the city, it undoubtedly does not seem much of a tourist haunt."

Without another word she attacked her custard tart without enthusiasm. The sweet had no taste as she swallowed back her tears of disappointment, not only over the death of her adventure, but over Devon's mercurial change into a martinet. Neither the general nor Margate had ever spoken to her in such a manner. She knew she was impetuous at times, but she certainly did not deserve to be dressed down so thoroughly over a simple question.

"Come, Ann-Louise, we shall retire now. I find that I am fatigued from the exertion of driving today," she announced, realizing that she could not stay in the room a minute longer without doing something foolish. She was not going to give Mr. Devon Delane the satisfaction of seeing her burst into angry tears or throw a temper tantrum. She would quietly go to her room and dwell on every horrible name and unspeakable torture she could think of for the pompous draper. How could she have ever considered that he was anything more than a common tradesman?

Her head was held high and her back straight as she walked across the room, Ann-Louise following behind like a faithful retainer. The grand exit was almost destroyed when Devon managed to reach the door ahead of her, holding it open with exaggerated courtesy. She nodded regally and sailed through the door, barely waiting for it to close behind her before she stomped up the stairs with her only friend at her heels.

"Now you've done it, lad," Margate murmured, lighting his pipe with an economy of motion, watching the younger man over the clay bowl.

Devon stood with his back to the closed door, seeming to need it for support. Slowly he let out his pent-up breath and allowed his body to begin to relax. "If looks could kill, my man, I would be a burnt cinder to be crushed under a certain young lady's heel, dust beneath her feet. For a moment I thought I would be skewered on her fork, but she decided to eat her sweet with it instead. Just how long does she usually stay angry?"

"When she starts talking like a starched-up matron lady, it could be days before she comes out of her sulks. Of course, if she thinks of a real good plan of revenge, she could be right as rain in the morning."

"Revenge?" The word stopped Devon from raising his glass to his lips. After hesitating a moment, he tossed back the contents. "What do you mean by revenge?"

"The miss doesn't get mad like most people, hollering

and putting up a fuss. She goes off by herself, plotting and scheming over the matter," Margate explained as he lolled back in his chair, puffing on his pipe as if he did not have a single care in the world. "Tomorrow morning you'll be able to tell if she's come up with a suitable means of paying you back. If she's still having a case of the sullens, there's nothing to worry about, but if she's cheerful and chattering at her usual pace, then you'd best head for cover."

"All this because I will not let her go into town?" Devon ran his hand through his hair without realizing what he had done. He thought he understood women until a few days ago; however, each day Joslyn Penderton showed him that he knew absolutely nothing.

"It's not so much ruining her chance to explore, it's how you said it. The general fairly doted on the girl and was never much on scolding her, and you've met the mother." He shrugged as if that was sufficient information about Lady Amelia. "I've been somewhat remiss myself, usually letting her have her own way as long as it didn't harm anyone. Didn't I agree to come on this lark with her?"

"For her own protection. And I had to do it. You know I have to meet with the lieutenant to see if our Mr. Heaton has returned to town," Devon said in his defense, wondering why he felt like such an ogre for doing what had to be done. Pacing the room, he expended his restlessness, so he would not be tempted to run up the stairs and apologize to Joslyn. "Can you imagine what Joslyn would do if she discovered there was some real intrigue afoot? She would be in the thick of it, trying to help me catch Heaton and his cronies."

"Don't let it eat at you, lad. It is past time that the miss learns that she can't have her own way every time. This is only a minor setback." The old man leaned forward and refilled Devon's glass. "She's going to be in a royal snit when she finds out who you are and that she won't be setting up house by herself in London."

Devon groaned and stopped in mid-stride as he visualized the scene. It would be an uncomfortable interview indeed. If he was this cut up over Joslyn's anger, how was he going to manage their inevitable confrontation over her engagement? Had the general had any idea what he was getting Devon into by asking him to look after his family? Sitting down at the table again, he picked up his glass. "Margate, you should have left me lying in the road that day—it would have been better for all concerned."

Joslyn measured the length of the room in angry strides, then turned to repeat her steps for the twentieth time. Ann-Louise sat patiently in front of the fire, her head cocked to the side, waiting for her mistress to settle down. Joslyn was in the mood for activity, however, even pacing the small confines of her room. How dare that blackguard reprimand her behavior?

She would show him that she was responsible and knew how to take care of herself. There must be some means for her to travel into town without Mr. Devon Delane's superior guidance. That was it! She would prove to him that she could take care of herself. He did not have to spare a moment of his precious time watching over her like some brooding hen. The only question was, how could she accomplish it?

A scraping at the door interrupted her list of possible escapes. Was it Devon coming to apologize? Walking to the door, she dismissed the hopeful thought immediately. In his present Calvinist frame of mind, he would not be seeking an audience with an unattended female. When she opened the door, she discovered she was correct. Her caller was the smiling maid who brought her water before dinner, Tully's sister.

"Yes? It's Dulcie, isn't it?"

"Aye, mum, I broughts yer bedwarmer. The handsome gent said ya was ready ta sleep." The girl bobbed quickly, then hesitated when the lady still stood in the doorway. Perhaps she had misunderstood, since the lady was still fully dressed.

"Oh, yes, of course," Joslyn replied thoughtfully, stepping back to allow the girl into the room. She continued to study the girl as she went about her business, filling the warming pan and expertly running it between the sheets. Dulcie was about her height and only weighed a few more pounds, so perhaps her clothes would fit. It would not be men's clothing, but it would be a disguise.

"Twill there be anythin' else, mum?"

"Dulcie, come sit by the fire for a moment," Joslyn invited with a gentle smile. The girl seemed hesitant but intrigued by the request. "I would like to ask you some questions about traveling into town."

6

"Here, what's this?" Margate exclaimed when he opened the door the next morning. Though it was half-past ten, he had not been out of his bed long. Devon kept him from his sleep for most of the night, full of plans—and a quantity of wine—expounding on how he would be handling Joslyn's future.

The last person he expected to find at his door was the young miss. She stood framed in the doorway, holding a tray bearing a teapot, a mug and a napkin-covered plate in front of her like a shield. A sunny smile stretched across her round face as she waited for him to stand aside.

"This is your morning tea, sir," Joslyn returned, her smile never wavering when he moved to let her enter the room. The men's quarters were bigger than her cubicle, but just as sparsely furnished. One quarter of the room had a sloping ceiling where the roof cut away near the chimney. Walking briskly to the fireplace, she stood in front of a faded, overstuffed chair until Margate joined her. "I have come to make my peace, though Dulcie says that Devon has already gone. So I shall just have to make my apologies twice."

"What are you up to, miss? I didn't see as much as a flinch when you uttered the word apology," he stated suspiciously, but sat down in the chair and allowed her to fuss over him. She placed the tray securely on his lap and

79

made a great ceremony of pouring his tea. Finally, she whipped the napkin off the plate to reveal buttered scones.

"The pair of you are much tidier than I am," she began, sitting in the chair across from him to teeter on the edge of the cushion. Surveying the room with interest, she folded her hands primly at the top of her knees. She looked everywhere, except at the old gentleman sitting directly in her line of vision. "So, how was Devon this morning? Was he nervous about facing his ogre of an employer? The man certainly could not sack him because of a silly accident."

Margate did not answer, but simply took another sip of his tea. His eyes took in every detail of his companion's appearance and attitude. "Did I hear someone mention the word apology?"

"Well, as to that, I suppose Devon is the one who deserves to hear my apology. After all, he was the one I turned on like a vicious shrew."

"You're much too hard on yourself, miss. You were only a trifle up in the boughs, not playing Lady MacWhat's-it that murdered all those people," the old man said quietly. He had trouble keeping his lips from turning into a smile at her self-effacing manner.

"You're thinking of Lady MacBeth, and she nagged at her husband to do her vile deeds, I think. No matter," she returned, dismissing literature from the conversation without a second's thought. "When will Devon be returning?"

"He didn't say exactly. Was there something in particular you wanted to see him about, or was it just that apology?"

"Must you keep harping on my apology? I admit that I behaved badly, especially after Devon has been so kind to offer his help in escaping from Gervais." Joslyn straightened the skirt of her blue cambric dress unnecessarily. She knew what she had to do, but now that the time was at hand, she was hesitant about carrying it through. But it was already too late to back down, so she had to press on.

"Devon didn't expect to be back much before supper, which he had asked to be served around six o'clock. Does that fit into your schedule, miss?"

Margate was watching her so closely that Joslyn was

afraid to even blink, lest he begin to suspect she was plotting something. "Schedule? I have no schedule, other than taking Ann-Louise out for an airing occasionally. Remember, Devon said I am to stay at the inn, nice and safe and out of trouble."

"Just so you remember that that is the plan," Margate said, nodding his head for emphasis. Then he shook his head, seeming to have trouble keeping his eyes open. Sitting up very straight, he directed a stern look at his young charge. "What have you done, girl?"

Joslyn jumped to her feet and pulled the tray off Margate's lap as his head lolled to rest on the side of the chair. She stood staring at him in rapt fascination as his eyes flickered shut, and a minute later he began to snore. She wondered how Devon had managed to sleep amid such a racket the previous night. Then her shoulders sagged in relief as she murmured an answer to Margate's last question. "I put a few drops of laudanum in your tea. You will have a nice nap, safely locked in your room until Tully comes to let you out, as I have instructed."

Halfway across the room, she realized that she was tiptoeing and gave a nervous giggle at the unnecessary precaution. Devon had been gone for two hours, according to Dulcie, and Margate would be asleep for some time. Tully would check on the old man long after Joslyn had gone. There was no need for stealth. She was free as a bird to show Devon that she could take care of herself. Then why was she letting a trace of guilt eat at her as she turned the key in the lock?

Shaking off her feeling of unease, Joslyn hurried back to her room. Ann-Louise sprang up from her place by the cold grate as her mistress rushed into the room. The dog eagerly waited while the young lady deposited the tray on the bed next to the parasol and shawl that were laid out. Joslyn did not give her pet a second thought, however. She had to be in the stable yard by eleven as Dulcie instructed her, or else Gantry would leave for town without her.

A whimper from Ann-Louise stopped Joslyn as she reached for the doorknob. With a sigh of frustration she turned and retraced her steps. She crouched down so that she was face to face with her pet's woeful brown eyes. "You *shtupid* beast, I cannot take you with me today. Tully will be along shortly to take you for a nice, long walk. Be a good girl, and I shall have a special treat for you at dinner."

After a last consoling scratch behind Ann-Louise's ear, Joslyn scrambled to her feet. She had to make haste, or all her careful plans would be for naught. Dulcie had been heavensent last night with her news that her uncle made weekly trips into Manchester for supplies. Gantry also spent the afternoon swapping lies with his cronies at the White Bear, which Dulcie claimed was his real reason for not having the supplies delivered. Joslyn would have plenty of time to explore the town and possibly discover the office of her father's solicitor.

"There ya be, young lady. I was about ta leave without ya," shouted Gantry from the driver's seat of his wagon. "Hop up behind with Dulcie, then we be off."

Joslyn barely had time to scramble onto the back of the wagon before Gantry sprang the horses. Luckily the draft horses were as sluggish as Cornwallis, and she had plenty of time to settle herself beside the other girl.

"Did ya really give the old gent a dose of laudanum? I don't think I could have done such a thing," Dulcie whispered eagerly once Joslyn was securely in place.

"Yes, I did. Will Tully remember to let Margate out in a few hours?" Joslyn asked as she tried to catch her breath. She did not care to admit that she had been reluctant to go through with her marvelous plan.

"Aye, he'll do it all right. I told him it was for the pretty lady, and he was anxious ta help," the girl confided. "He doesn't seem ta care for that brother of yours. Says he's awful toplofty for a common gent."

"My brother? Oh, Devon is a very good brother," Joslyn replied, suddenly remembering what had been said to Herbert Gantry the previous night. "He is just accustomed to having his own way."

Not wanting to dwell on the subject of Devon, Joslyn quickly began firing questions at her unsuspecting accomplice. Poor Dulcie thought Joslyn wanted to go into town to buy a present for her brother as a surprise. The girl was simple enough not to wonder why it was necessary to drug the old gent to accomplish the mission, and Joslyn did not see any need to explain any more than was necessary. What mattered was that she was going into Manchester, and had managed to do the deed herself with no help from Mr. Devon Delane.

By mid-afternoon, however, Joslyn was beginning to wonder if there had not been some sense in what Devon had said. Manchester was dirty, crowded, and hot. Her earlier enchantment with the mortar-and-timber buildings and winding, narrow streets had quickly disappeared once Gantry set them down to explore on foot. Dulcie's incessant chatter, which always seemed to circle back to Devon, was beginning to strain Joslyn's nerves. The last person she wanted to talk or even think about was Devon—especially after the close call she had had when Dulcie was escorting her around the stalls of the market not a half-hour past.

"Look, isn't that your brother across the square?" the girl had called in a clear, ringing voice. A number of heads had turned their way, inspecting the young lady and her noisy companion.

"Oh, heavens, Dulcie, he cannot see me," Joslyn returned, looking around in agitation for a place to hide. She stepped back in the shadow of a tarpaulin hanging behind a jeweler's booth. Her caution was not necessary, however, as Devon was deep in conversation with the gentleman at his side, never turning his head in Joslyn's direction.

The two men continued up the street and entered an establishment that bore the sign of Heaton's Linens. Joslyn had to ignore the sour feeling in the pit of her stomach as she acknowledged that Devon truly was a draper after all. How could she have been foolish enough to think he was anything but what he said he was? He had certainly told her often enough, so why had she tried so hard to imagine he was something different?

"I think that bloke is following us." Dulcie's indignant

whisper brought Joslyn back to the present. For once the girl had lowered her voice to a reasonable tone.

"Perhaps he has taken a fancy to you, Dulcie," Joslyn replied absently, wondering how soon they could join the girl's uncle and return to the inn. Her feet hurt, her limbs ached all over, and she was hungry. She had forgotten about bringing some money, which would have meant rifling Margate's pockets. Her only food since breakfast was a hot cross bun that she and Dulcie shared. Fortunately Dulcie did not question how Joslyn planned to purchase a present for her brother without a half-penny in her pocket.

"I'd rather have some drunken coachman pestering me than have that cove come near me," Dulcie announced with loathing. "He looks ta be a right nasty one."

"What?" The edge of distaste in the girl's voice captured Joslyn's attention. She looked in the direction that Dulcie was staring, but could not discern which man she was talking about in the milling crowd. "Where is this man?"

"He's right over there— Now that's right strange. He disappeared." Dulcie seemed almost disappointed that the menacing stranger was no longer in sight. "He was standing not three feet from here, staring at us as bold as ya please."

"Have you ever seen him before?" Joslyn was more than curious now. What was it about the man that had agitated Dulcie so?

"No, I'd have remembered an ugly customer the likes of him. He was acting sort of havey-cavey with his hat pulled down over his face, almost like he didn't want ta be seen." Dulcie's words dwindled away as her expression suddenly became alert, and she started to laugh.

"What are you laughing about? Certainly not that horrible man you saw," Joslyn asserted, and wished once more that she was back at the inn. She could have stayed in her room with her feet up all day, playing the lady of leisure, and only venturing out of doors with Ann-Louise every few hours.

"I'm laughing at meself, of course. That cove weren't interested in us, but looking at the lay of land for some likely pockets ta pick," the girl explained, still chuckling over her mistake. "My ma says I'm too vain for my own good sometimes, but I've never got so carried away ta worry that a cut-purse had taken a fancy ta me."

"Well, I suppose we should be heading back to the White Bear to find your uncle," Joslyn put in hopefully. This adventure had become so ordinary. She had done nothing in Manchester that she could not do at home in Dukinfield. The streets here were narrower and more crowded ten times over, as well as dusty and dank. Worst of all, she still had not remembered the direction of her father's solicitor, only that it was on some square. Dulcie had been quick to point out there were any number of squares in town, and she never had need of a lawyer of any kind, so she did not know which location would be most likely.

"Right ya are, miss. Uncle Herbert will be wanting ta go as soon as he gets the notion," Dulcie replied and headed off at a brisk pace in the direction of the inn, with Joslyn skipping to keep up with her.

The sight of the dormer windows of the Bonnie Prince looked like heaven to Joslyn more than an hour later. Gantry had been deep in conversation with his cronies when Joslyn and Dulcie had reached the White Bear. He was out of sorts at being interrupted, and made the pair wait until he was good and ready to leave. Though Joslyn longed for something cool to drink, she had not dared make the request, lest Gantry refuse to transport her back to his inn.

"Why, there's that bloke again," Dulcie announced the minute she jumped down from the wagon. The yard of the Bonnie Prince seemed to be full of people and horses as the mail coach was getting ready to depart.

"What man?" Joslyn asked with little interest. She was already contemplating a soothing bath before the fire, no matter what the extra cost to Devon.

"That sneak thief from the market in town. He's harried off again, like a blessed ghost, so there's something havey-cavey about him all right," Dulcie determined, but Joslyn had already lost interest and was heading for the door. "I'd best let uncle know there's a cut-purse on the loose."

Joslyn was not attending because she was considering

turning around and walking all the way back to Manchester. The sight that greeted her weary eyes the minute she entered the inn was Devon, pacing back and forth at the bottom of the stairs. Thanks to Dulcie's piercing voice behind her, their entrance did not go unnoticed. Joslyn had no chance to escape and sneak up to her room by another route.

Devon stopped in mid-stride, turning quickly on his heels to face the doorway, and unerringly located Joslyn's quiet figure. He did not speak, but it was not necessary. His brown eyes were almost black with rage, his face flushed with emotion. A shiver of apprehension skated down Joslyn's spine as she stood frozen in place. The previous night's lecture seemed mild compared to his current barely suppressed anger. Until that moment, she foolishly had not considered how Devon would react to her bid for independence.

Hesitantly she took a step forward, wondering why her feet would not cooperate and carry her back out the front door to relative safety. She was sure that Devon would be able to catch her before she managed to reach the roadway. With another step she noticed that Devon was no longer wearing his sling; both hands were at his side, clenched into tight fists at the moment. Was that what was keeping him from reaching for her throat? There was repressed violence in his stormy eyes. He had not looked this dangerous even when he had faced their intruder at the lodge.

"Hello, Devon, how was your day?" Her voice came out as a bare thread of sound. Since he did not see fit to reply, she cleared her throat and tried again, her fingers nervously twisting the fringe of her shawl. "Was your employer very upset, er, anxious about your absence?"

She wanted to sink in the planked floor beneath her feet. *Of all the shtupid things to say*, she chastised herself, before realizing fatalistically that nothing she said would be appropriate. Devon still did not respond, but walked forward in two long strides until they were toe-to-toe.

"The parlor, young lady."

His voice was low and urgent, heard only by Joslyn, who

marvelled that his lips had not moved an inch. She considered answering him for a moment, going so far as to part her lips, but one more look at his grim face brought her to her senses. Ducking her head, she walked slowly down the hallway to the private parlor as he had ordered.

Devon watched her move away, not trusting himself to speak or move for the moment. He had never experienced such fear as the moment he returned to the inn and discovered that Joslyn had gone to Manchester alone. Facing a line of charging French cavalry seemed to be child's play in comparison. What had he ever done to deserve Joslyn Penderton in his life?

Taking measured steps toward the parlor, he counseled himself to remain calm and in control. He was the adult, the superior intellect. He had to forget the giddiness of relief he had felt the minute she walked through the door, looking as if she had been out for an afternoon stroll. The feeling had been quickly followed by an irrational anger that she was safe and unharmed. He had wanted to hug her and spank her at the same time. But, above all else, he must remain cool and composed.

"Have you taken leave of your senses, young lady? Or were you born without any brains at all?" he stormed the second he slammed the door behind him. The flow of his tirade was not deterred by the startled green eyes that stared at him in fascination. "Do you want that oafish cousin of yours to find you? Well, I am beginning to think he is welcome to you, and if he were here at this moment, I would hand you to him myself."

Joslyn stood in the middle of the room, not saying a word or moving a muscle. She seemed to be afraid to move or speak, on the chance Devon would do something violent. He certainly felt like smashing crockery or breaking a chair in two. "What do I have to do to make you behave yourself? I thought I could trust you to have enough sense to stay out of trouble. But, no, what do you do? You drug a defenseless old man and run off on a lark, and to what purpose? You had to have your own way. And it was not just yourself that you embroiled in this affair, but two innocent children as well."

"Is Margate all right? It was just a little laudanum," Joslyn finally managed to whisper, still clutching the ends of her shawl.

"I should tell you that he is deathly ill, just to teach you a lesson, but he is perfectly all right. He has been worrying himself needlessly on your behalf most of the afternoon, however. Are you proud of yourself? Did you enjoy your little junket?" Devon planted his fists on his hips, and tapped his foot while he waited for her reply.

She did not want to answer his questions, torn between telling the truth and salvaging her pride. Finally, she gave up, her body sagging in the relief of admitting the truth. "No."

"No?" The single word caught Devon by surprise, which was not unusual when he was dealing with Joslyn. "What do you mean, no?"

"No, I am not proud of myself, and no, I did not enjoy myself," she shot back in an almost unintelligible mutter. Lifting her head to look at him square in the eye, she raised her chin and asked, "Are you satisfied, sir?"

"Oh, Joslyn, what am I going to do with you?" Devon said more to himself than to the girl who was valiantly trying to hold back her tears. He closed the space between them in one stride, ready to draw her into his arms to comfort her. Joslyn seemed to shy away, however, so he settled for placing his hands lightly on her shoulders.

"Joslyn, I am sorry I yelled at you, but you scared both Margate and me out of five years of our lives. I did not tell you to stay here to ruin your day," he said gently, hoping to repair some of the damage caused by his foul temper. He could not tell her the real reason for his fears, so he would have to make do with her cousin as an excuse. "If you want to stay free of your cousin and his scheming mother, you will have to do as I say."

"You could have explained this to me earlier, instead of demanding that I do what you wanted," she replied with a hint of aggression. She hated being given orders, even if it was for her own good. Why could she not have some say about her own life? No one bothered to consider her feelings, just her behavior, when they made decisions for her. That is exactly what her papa had done by giving her hand to Captain Farraday without her consent.

"There is not always time to give explanations, imp. I might have explained last night if you had given me time before you made your grand exit," Devon stated, giving her an ingratiating smile, then daring to chuck her under the chin with knuckle.

Oh, why does everyone treat me like a child, Joslyn wondered while giving Devon a weak smile in return. *He simply does not understand*, she thought sadly, but decided against making an issue of the matter. He was a man and could not understand what it was like to have no control over one's life. She would have to bide her time and hope she could explain the matter to him later, when both of them were less emotional. For now she wanted that bath she had been imagining since mid-day, and now she hoped it did cost Devon extra.

Dinner was a quiet affair, since no one was certain of a safe topic of conversation. After a number of abortive attempts to rouse Joslyn from her silence, Devon gave up. He spent his time discussing the next day's traveling arrangements with Margate. Even mentioning that he should be able to drive the cart did not get a rise out of the young lady as expected.

"Tomorrow you shall have an ally against my domineering ways, imp," Devon stated, his tone much harder than his feelings. He could not bear to see Joslyn so cast down. Her bright, illogical chatter had enlivened the past days, and he discovered he sorely missed it.

"Surely no one else has been so forward to bring that to your notice," she responded with some of her previous spirit, a ghost of a smile on her lips.

"Now don't be impertinent to the gentleman, miss." Margate joined in the spirit of the banter after a speaking look from Devon. He was rewarded by Joslyn wrinkling her nose in disgust.

"My mother and my aunt Joan have always been more

than eager to countermand any of my suggestions," Devon continued, his mood lightening at the promising beginning. "Neither of them can seem to remember that I am no longer in the schoolroom, especially my aunt. I am sure she will enlighten you with the day I brought mud pies to her elegant garden parties."

Ann-Louise did not seem to find the comment as amusing as the others. The small dog left her post by Devon's side to trot to the door, then waited expectantly for someone to notice her.

"It seems that we shall have to continue this after a brief interruption," Joslyn announced and placed her napkin on the table. She pulled Ann-Louise's leash from her pocket, but kept it concealed in her skirt until she reached the door. "Do not worry, Devon, we shall only go to the edge of the stables. I have learned my lesson against rebellion for the day."

"You didn't have any luck today, m'lord, if we're leaving in the morning," Margate asked as soon as the miss had closed the door securely behind her. In all the commotion over Joslyn's disappearance earlier, there had been no chance to discuss Devon's mission.

"Heaton was not in when we stopped at his shop this afternoon. McCrory is going to stay in Manchester and keep an eye on the place while I escort our charge to my aunt's house. We still have not determined who is behind hoarding the coins, since McCrory's revenuers have found no connection in Liverpool. At this point the money is still in Manchester." The younger man lounged back in his chair, twirling his wine glass between his finger and studying the play of the candlelight on its smooth surface. "Joslyn seems to be taking our little skirmish rather well. Or am I being optimistic?"

"I'm not sure. She was very quiet just now, but I think she's right about learning a valuable lesson today," Margate stated between bites of his stew. He chewed thoughtfully for a moment, then continued. "She admitted that she'd done something silly, and that is something rare. Usually she thinks she's in the right, no matter what anyone has to say."

"I shall be content just as long as she does not go wandering off by herself again," Devon returned before refilling his glass and helping himself to another portion of stew from the tureen in the middle of the table. Guardianship was a weary business and seemed to increase his appetite. "I hope to get this business with Heaton cleared up in the next fortnight. Once that is settled, we shall tackle a more dangerous adversary, our Joslyn."

Joslyn stood on the front step, staring sightlessly off toward the horizon. She felt a momentary twinge of regret at her churlish words before leaving the parlor, but dismissed it. Surely she had some right to an opinion occasionally; Devon did not have to have the upper hand all the time.

The deserted yard in front of her was cloaked in shadows, since there was no moon. Ann-Louise was impatient with her mistress's woolgathering and strained at her leash. When it did not rouse Joslyn, the dog decided a bark or two might be justified. A rustling in the bushes distracted her from her human's lack of response.

"Oh, Ann-Louise, are you going to chastise me as well?" Joslyn asked with a short laugh, allowing her pet to pull her in the direction of the stables. "I have been counting on you to be my ally and, if necessary, to take a nice piece out of Devon's leg the next time he decides to play the Little Dictator. Although I suppose he is too tall to actually impersonate the emperor."

Ann-Louise was much too busy sniffing at the ground to answer, and Joslyn was content to follow her lead. A sudden breeze made her wish she had not left her shawl behind in the parlor. The stable door shielded her a little from the cool night air, but it also cut off the light from the lantern hanging over the door. Much as she hated to admit it, Joslyn wished she had asked Devon to accompany her.

The next moment she let out a gasp of surprise as an arm grasped her around the waist. Then she became angry as she realized who had snuck up behind her. "Devon, this is not funny. I learned my lesson about running off, so stop this nonsense."

He did not stop, merely clamped a hand over her mouth at the same moment Ann-Louise turned back to see what was keeping her mistress. The dog let out a low, fierce growl that made Joslyn realize that the man holding her was not Devon.

7

"STOP that dog's yapping, or it'll bring the whole inn down on us," a voice growled close to Joslyn's ear, keeping her from moving. He kept one hand over her mouth while holding her firmly around the waist with his right arm. His tight grip pinned her arms to her sides and raised her feet off the ground.

A curse answered him from the darkness. "Bloody beast bit me!"

Joslyn's assailant gave a snort of laughter, as if amused by his companion's wound. "I already have that mongrel's mark on my leg. I'd as soon shoot it as muzzle it."

As his words sank in, Joslyn began to struggle in earnest. This was the man from the lodge, but what did he want with her? She had no money on her person, nor was she an heiress who could be held for ransom. Had he mistaken her for someone else? Or could her aunt have hired these henchmen to track her down instead of Gervais?

"Damn, she's a lively one. Where's the bag? I can't hold her much longer." The man broke off with a curse as Joslyn managed to land a blow to his shin with the heel of her foot. His hand slipped from her mouth, and she gathered much needed air into her lungs. But before she could utter a sound, a cloth was stuffed into her mouth, cutting off her cry for help.

She was not going to go quietly, no matter how fast her

heart was racing or how much she was trembling. There were two men, so she would have to break away quickly, hoping to delay them long enough for someone to come to her rescue. How long had she been gone? Would Devon come looking for her or think that Ann-Louise was in an investigative mood? If only she could stay calm.

"Haven't ya got that beast muzzled yet?" the man demanded, pushing Joslyn up against the side of the stable, immobilizing her against the wooden plank wall with his body. "Do I have to do everything? Isn't it enough I chased the girl all over the city today?"

"Aye, it's done," called the other man, his voice moving closer to the stable. "What'd ya do with the bag and the rope?"

"It's behind me somewhere, and put a rush on. I can't hold this hellion much longer without striking her, and the boss don't want her harmed yet."

Joslyn stopped struggling for a moment, stunned by the implications of his words. This must be the man Dulcie had seen following them today. What was happening? Why would this man appear at the lodge and in Manchester? How could he know where they were traveling? Did Devon know anything about this? Perhaps he was not a respectable draper after all, but nothing more than a smuggler. Did smugglers work so far inland?

She did not have time to reason out the matter. The man holding her had said he would actually hit a woman. She did not have a single weapon to defend herself. Unfortunately, her sudden stillness aided her assailants. Her tormentor held her arms at her sides while the other man trussed her from her shoulders to her knees. She tried to wiggle to impede them, but it was futile. Something coarse and foul smelling was dragged over her head and pulled down her body, where they secured it with more rope. She was sightless and powerless as one of the men bound her ankles.

The world spun around her for a moment before Joslyn realized she was being tossed over one of the men's shoulders. "I got her now. You take the dog," the man ordered, walking unsteadily under the weight of his burden.

He ignored the other man's coarse response to the order. "We'll let the beast go a ways down the road with a note for our friend. We don't want him on our trail too soon."

Joslyn tried to mutter every foul word she could think of and make dire threats, but only succeeded in making grunting noises through the cloth and the bag. She tried to scream her outrage as the man suddenly flung her in the air, and she landed with a resounding thud on something hard and unyielding. Her body was going to be one massive bruise before the night was over. The creak of leather and the strong smell of horse and hay told her what had occurred. She had been thrown into the back of a wagon.

As the wagon began to move, she could hear Ann-Louise whimpering from somewhere above her head. She wanted to cry herself, but knew it was a useless effort. There were more important matters to consider, she told herself sternly, trying to brace herself against the side of the wagon. How was she going to get away from these men? She did not know where they were taking her, or why.

While she was jostled from side to side as the wagon picked up speed, another thought began to plague her. Would Devon want to come to her rescue after her foolish behavior today?

"Did Miss Joslyn go up to bed already, sir? Should I take her dessert up to her?" Dulcie asked as she began clearing away the table, giving Devon her best smile.

Where was Joslyn? Devon had not realized how long she had been gone until Dulcie came into the room. What was his reluctant betrothed up to this time? Apparently he had relaxed much too soon, becoming overconfident at her docile behavior earlier. With a feeling of resignation, he got to his feet. "Margate, I am going out to see what is keeping Joslyn."

"Don't get too excited, lad. She is probably just off dreaming, or that silly beast is pretending to be a real dog, ferreting out some game," the older man stated, not upset by Joslyn's absence. He seemed more interested in the apple crumble that Dulcie placed in front of him. "The miss can stand for hours just woolgathering, without a thought to anyone else on earth."

"I shall feel better if I check just the same," Devon called over his shoulder. How could one girl be more trouble than the entire French army or a whole band of smugglers? Life had never been this uncertain during his army days, and he had spent more time in the past twenty-four hours worrying over Joslyn than the felonious Mr. Heaton.

When he found the yard deserted, Devon turned toward the stables, muttering under his breath about irresponsible children. He had to think of Joslyn as an obstreperous child. If he did not, he found himself dwelling on the beauty of her eyes, or the fascinating dimple that would suddenly appear at the corner of her mouth when she laughed. These were not the thoughts of a responsible guardian.

"Were ya needin' me, sir?" chirruped a hesitant voice from behind him. Devon spun around to confront the new arrival, who was trotting across the yard from the back of the inn.

"Have you seen Jos— my sister, boy? She brought her dog out for a walk not long ago." Devon snapped out the words without considering the boy's feelings. He needed to know where Joslyn had gone. At the youngster's wary look, however, he tried to approach the matter more reasonably. "My sister has been gone for a long time, and I am worried that something has happened to her, Tully. It is Tully, isn't it?"

The boy nodded, but still looked slightly apprehensive. He shuffled his feet from side to side as if trying to decide what to answer. "Tain't seen Miss Joslyn since the mornin', sir. Been in the kitchen gettin' my dinner. Didn't see nobody in the yard."

Devon gave him a searching look to assure himself the boy was telling the truth. Joslyn had enchanted the lad since the moment they arrived, and it was possible—despite Devon's lecture earlier—that she might have another scheme afoot. Tully seemed to sense his intent and matched Devon's stare with a pugnacious glare.

The child's defiance satisfied Devon that he had spoken

the truth. Almost irrationally he wished that the boy was lying, and Joslyn was plotting some prank. A prickly feeling at the back of his neck told him that something was terribly amiss. It was the same feeling he always experienced just before battle. Had what he had been dreading come to pass? Could Heaton suspect that Devon wasn't a common merchant?

Without another thought to the boy, Devon began to walk back to the inn, his footsteps picking up speed the closer he came to the building. By the time he reached the entrance, he was running. Racing into the entry, he headed for the stairs and climbed them two at a time. He was out of breath by the time he reach Joslyn's room, giving little thought to proper behavior as he thrust open the door.

Just as he feared; the room was empty. He turned on his heels to return belowstairs, not bothering to close the door behind him. Ann-Louise's bark sounded from the front of the inn before he was halfway down the stairs. Jumping down the last three steps, he spotted her immediately. She sat framed in the front door, her tongue lolling out the side of her mouth, and she was taking shallow breaths as if she had been running for miles.

Devon barely noticed that Margate had joined him in the entry. He did not hesitate and rushed forward, hoping Joslyn was following close behind her pet. The old man was at his heels, looking hopefully over his shoulder as he searched the deserted yard of the inn. Devon turned and met Margate's grim expression, but did not speak before he bent to inspect the spaniel. Her fur was damp from her exertions, littered with twigs and leaves.

"What's the matter, lass? Where's Joslyn?" Margate said softly as he bent over the pair. His tone was gentle, at odds with his normal brisk manner with the animal.

Ann-Louise only whimpered in response, looking from one man to the other. Both Devon and Margate knew she held the key to Joslyn's disappearance, but were frustrated by the inability to communicate. Devon quickly rose to his feet, causing Ann-Louise to give a low growl. "I shall commandeer a horse— Damn it, what's got into her?"

Ann-Louise was throwing herself against his leg, barking and growling to get his attention. Then she stopped her frenzied attack as quickly as she began. Sitting on her haunches, she began scratching behind her ear with her back leg.

"Joslyn has vanished and the beast is worried about fleas," Devon muttered in disgust, trying to think of a rational explanation for what was happening. The spaniel's condition told him that this was not an innocent prank, but something deadly serious.

"It's not fleas, lad. There's something stuck under her collar, and she's trying to work it loose," Margate shot back, suddenly looking every one of his sixty-odd years. He bent from the waist, his balance precarious with his arm still in the sling, but he pulled the cloth packet from Ann-Louise's collar without mishap. The dog barked her encouragement as he straightened.

Devon was too impatient to wait for the older man to open the packet. He snatched it from Margate's hand, noting for the first time that the man was trembling. His own fingers were unsteady as he fumbled with the oilcloth.

"Be there a problem, sir?" Herbert Gantry called from behind him just as Devon pulled back the cloth to reveal a folded piece of paper.

Devon wanted to curse at the interruption. He handed the packet to Margate and turned to smile at the innkeeper. For the first time, he noticed a small crowd had gathered at the entrance to the public room. Curious faces were watching him, waiting patiently for a logical explanation for his mad dash up and down the stairs, as well as Ann-Louise's performance.

"Nothing is wrong, Mr. Gantry. I am so sorry we disturbed your guests," Devon began, wondering wildly how he was going to disperse the crowd without arousing everyone's suspicions. "It was a wager. Yes, a wager. I bet my man here that the stupid beast would not be able to carry a message from the stables without losing it."

He held his breath, waiting for the group's response. Did they think his story was as lame as it sounded to his ears?

Apparently not, he thought with relief and let out his breath. After a few disappointed looks, and a few of disgust, the men went back to their own business.

Devon gave Gantry a jaunty salute and turned to Margate. "Come, Margate, you deserve another ale to celebrate your victory. I shall have Dulcie bring us another round, or possibly two. Come, Ann-Louise."

He strolled down the hall to the parlor as if he did not have a care in the world. With each step he had to force himself to keep a sedate pace, never giving in to the temptation to look over his shoulder where Margate was behind him with the precious letter that Ann-Louise delivered.

Finally he was in the parlor, Margate and Ann-Louise coming close behind in orderly fashion. Devon grimaced at the spectacle they must have made parading into the private room, but quickly threw off his chagrin as Margate handed him the oilcloth packet.

He tossed aside the wrapping and opened the letter, dreading that it was something more than a letter from Joslyn's relations. At first the scrawled words seemed to all run together, making only a jumble of letters. Devon steadied himself by taking a deep breath, and began reading again.

"What is it, lad? What's happened to the miss?" Margate's anxious questions were punctuated by a sharp bark from Ann-Louise. She started dancing around the men's feet, as though it would goad them to action.

"Heaton has taken her! He says she is his collateral in our business dealings," Devon stated flatly. Suddenly his body was drained of all feeling, except a growing sense of helplessness and despair. What had he done by involving Joslyn in his life? He was a fool, a complete idiot, to think his presence was all that was needed to keep her safe. She would have been much better off if she had never met him.

"Come on, man, what does he want?"

Devon roused himself from the morass of his recriminations at Margate's sharp words. He was not helping Joslyn by standing here acting like some character from a third-rate tragedy.

"There's nothing else. I am to stay at the inn until more instructions are sent at his convenience," Devon snarled, crumbling the paper in his hand and jumping to his feet. He was not going to sit here like some tame lap dog while Joslyn was being held prisoner.

"Very impressive, lad, but you're beginning to repeat yourself," Margate said quietly from behind him. "It is very nice indeed, but it doesn't solve our problem."

Until the old man spoke, Devon had not realized he had been pacing the room and muttering every invective he had learned during his military tour, in English, Portuguese, and French. Margate was right. Though his ranting relieved his taut nerves, it would not help to get Joslyn back.

"I am going to fetch McCrory and his men. You wait here in case our friend sends us another directive." He barked the orders as he headed for the door, only to be brought up short as he reached for the latch.

"Hold on, lad. We don't know if the bloke is watching the place. He might be waiting to see what you're about."

"Damn." Devon knew he was right, but he had to do something, anything, to set a plan in motion. "We cannot sit on our hands while the villain takes the upper hand."

"That's true, but we aren't without our troops," Margate began and gestured for Devon to take a seat. The younger man's agitation was helping him overcome his own apprehensions. Clear heads were needed to rescue the miss. "Call in that boy, Tully. He'll do anything to help his lady fair."

"We cannot involve a child in this," Devon shot back, then seemed to reconsider. "I see your point. The boy can get to McCrory without arousing suspicion. Margate, you are a good man to have around in a crisis. Ring for Dulcie to fetch the boy while I write a message to McCrory." Devon sprang to his feet and headed for the desk at the far end of the room, unaware of the interested look from his companion.

Though Margate was worried about his young charge, he found his lordship's actions very revealing, and somewhat amusing. The young man was head over heels in love with the miss, and was not even aware of it. Since he was a fairly bright fellow, Margate was sure Devon would come to understand his emotions before they had Joslyn safely back among them.

"Don't worry, lad, she'll be all right," Margate said softly, giving the bell pull a good tug to capture Dulcie's attention in the public room. "I'm not so sure we shouldn't be a little sorry for her kidnappers. They don't know what they've gotten themselves into by taking the miss."

"He hit me." Joslyn sat up, shaking her head and rubbing the sore spot on the back of her head. The beast had the gall to hit her, simply because she would not hold still when he took her out of the wretched wagon. She was bruised from shoulder to toe after that hideous ride, and that blackguard had the nerve to hit her. Apparently he had carried her to this dark, musty room and put her on this narrow cot while she was unconscious.

"Would you mind keepin' your voice down, I'm tryin' to sleep."

She jumped at the sound of the soft, drawling voice that came somewhere from the opposite side of the room. Though she was startled by the presence of another person, she swallowed a reflexive scream that formed in the back of her throat. The voice was cultured, unlike the men who had brought her here. This could be someone who could help her.

"Who are you? What is this place? Why have I been brought here?" she ventured, and swung her legs over the side of the cot. If she could get the person to speak again, perhaps she could locate him. She took a few tentative steps to assure herself that she could walk. Her eyes were slowly adjusting to the murky room, and she could make out some shapes that looked like trunks and chairs.

"Oh, you aren't goin' to be one of those chatterin' females, are you?" her mysterious companion asked in a plaintive tone. He was over to her right, but she still could not see him as she decided to hazard a few more cautious steps. "If you're goin' to be pesterin' me, I'll have to speak to Mr. Heaton about other accommodations."

"I am sorry, but I was brought here against my will and do not know where I am, or even why I am here." She was not about to be deterred by his querulous manner. This person with the strange, drawling accent was her only key to this mystery.

"I suppose I'm not goin' to get any sleep until you get settled," he muttered, and Joslyn heard the rustling sounds of movement. The next moment there was a scraping noise, and a light flared behind a massive shadow that turned into a jumble of tables and picture frames when illuminated. The light was moving from behind the furniture, then a lantern came into view held in the hand of a slender young man.

In the improved light, Joslyn could see that she was in a portion of the room that had been sectioned off from the rest. A partition of carefully spaced boards, like bars on a prison cell, divided the two sections. The young man was peering at her with narrowed eyes, then a smile illuminated his narrow face.

"Well, hello, hello. I must say, if I'd known I had such a pretty companion, I would not have waited before makin' my complaints," he stated with satisfaction. His smile grew wider as he ran his eyes over Joslyn's astonished face before traveling down the rest of her figure and back up to her face. "What did you say your name was? I'm Casimir Macdonald, late of North Carolina."

"North Carolina? Where is that, Ireland?"

"Beggin' your pardon, miss, but North Carolina is part of the United States of America." He stood up straight and puffed out his chest with this pronouncement, seeming almost offended by her poor knowledge of geography. "Now, what was your name?"

"You are from the colonies? But what are you doing in this . . . this . . . I suppose this is an attic," Joslyn murmured, looking around at the slanted roof line and unfinished walls.

"Do you or don't you have a name?"

The sharp words drew Joslyn's gaze back to the stranger.

He was not much older than she, possibly two or three years her senior. The scowl on his face emphasized his prominent nose and sloping forehead, topped by a thatch of ruffled blond hair. He was thin and shorter than Devon, and though he was dressed in a gentlemanly fashion, he did not wear his clothes with the same authority as Devon.

"Your name, please?" he asked again.

"Oh, I am so sorry. My name is Joslyn Penderton of Dukinfield, and I have been kidnapped," she stated matter-of-factly without trying to embellish the issue. She was not exactly sure how one was supposed to feel about a kidnapping, but she knew she was angry. How dare someone she did not know haul her off to this dusty hovel without telling her the reason? "Are you one of them, or are you another one of their helpless victims?"

"Victims? No, Mr. Heaton just said I was to stay here for a while after I missed my ship home. He was most accommodatin' in givin' me a place to stay. He's goin' to arrange for me to get passage on another ship," he announced in a confiding tone, but suddenly frowned as if considering his words. "He's takin' a considerable amount of time gettin' it done, though." Casimir seemed nonplussed by the thought and needed to mull over the matter.

Although she was impatient to question him further, Joslyn let him deliberate on the problem. She undoubtedly was not going to get very many answers from her new acquaintance, since the man did not even know how long he had been here. Were they victims of some kidnapping ring? Did kidnappers usually seize more than one person at a time? She certainly had never heard of any incident where groups of strangers had been held for ransom.

Rather than dwell on the riddle, Joslyn decided to explore her surroundings. Her companion was taking an unconscionable amount of time over a simple matter, and she had better things to do than watch him. She realized that there was not much to see as she turned in a circle where she stood. The soft light from the lantern only disclosed more old furniture and trunks that had been pushed aside to allow room for her cot and a washstand. From what she could see behind Casimir, his portion was the same.

"Say, I've been here for over a month," Casimir exclaimed, amazed by his discovery. "I must speak to Mr. Heaton about this matter. I think he should have found a ship to take me home by now, don't you?"

"I really could not say," she returned without concern for his transportation dilemma. The name Heaton was familiar, but she could not remember where she had heard it before, or why. She decided there were more important matters at hand, however, and the window on the far wall was her first priority.

She reached the outer wall in a few steps and groaned as she took a closer look at the glass. It was pitch black, not reflecting the dim light of Casimir's lantern. Bending closer, she felt a flare of hope. The panes were covered with dirt, so perhaps it was not shuttered on the outside. She grabbed the corner of a Holland cover that was draped over a square shape to her right and managed to wipe away a small circle of grime in the lower section.

Her victory was fleeting. There was not much to see outside, though she could tell it was still night. Apparently she had not been unconscious long; it must be the same evening that she had been taken from the Bonnie Prince. She knew she was in the city, because her prison was crowded among the dark shapes of other buildings. With a sigh of resignation, Joslyn stepped back and wiped her hands on the cloth.

Nothing could be discerned until daylight. By then Devon would come to her rescue, she hoped. A chill coursed over her skin as she remembered his stormy face when she had returned to the inn that afternoon. Did Devon think she had run away again? Would he think she was off on another selfish adventure and not bother to look for her?

Shaking off her apprehensive thoughts, Joslyn walked back to Casimir. She could not dwell on hysterical speculation. She had to think of a way to escape. Casimir was her only ally, and at the moment that was not a hopeful prospect, but she forged ahead. "Tell me about our host, Mr. Heaton. Who is he?"

Casimir seemed to brighten at the question, standing up straight and smiling again. This was apparently a subject that did not seem to tax his brain's capacity. "He is going to make me a king."

8

"I beg your pardon?" Joslyn could not believe she had heard him correctly. Too much had been happening in the last few hours, and she had a sudden desire to sit down. After looking around the immediate area, she sank down on a trunk that was relatively free of dust. "You did say a king?"

"That's what I said to Mr. Heaton when he first brought it up. I'm an American, I says, we don't have royalty anymore, had a war to stop that nonsense," Casimir informed her, pleased with his quick recall of recent history. With a calculating look at the distance between them, he suggested, "Why don't you take a seat over here, so I don't have to shout so much?"

She had not noticed that he was shouting, or even raising his voice, to converse, but she stood up and walked closer to the partition. Casimir grinned more broadly than before, if that was possible, and hastily bent to dust off a chair near an opening between the boards. The chair he selected was next to a matching one on his side of the divider. Once Joslyn was seated, he took his own chair and leaned companionably toward her.

"Now, isn't this much cozier? We can sit and chat like old friends," he stated, highly satisfied with the arrangement. "I haven't had much chance to talk to anyone, except Mr. Heaton and Wart."

"Wart?" Was this one of the men who brought her here? It would probably take another half hour for her to have Casimir describe the man, so she decided to keep to the topic of kings. She kept her hands firmly clasped in her lap, not sure she liked being this close to Casimir after all. His friendly demeanor was a trifle cloying at close range, and he seemed preoccupied with watching her hands.

"Wart's the one who brings my food since Mr. Heaton doesn't want me out wandering the street. He says he wants me close by, in case he finds a new ship to take me home."

"You said he was going to make you a king?" Joslyn prompted, hoping to discover some worthwhile information from this poor man's scattered wits.

"That's right, miss." He nodded vigorously to emphasize his point, then hesitated a moment, his eyes running over her from head to toe once more. "You wouldn't mind if I called you Joslyn, would you? I'm not sure how things are done over here, but it would be much friendlier if we used first names. You may call me Cas, like my friends at home."

"Thank you, Cas." She knew this was going to be rough going. Casimir seemed to think in an irregular manner, saying whatever came into his mind, never sticking to the point. How could she deal with someone who did not think logically? "Tell me about being a king."

"Well, Joslyn— What a lovely name. Has anyone ever told you that?" He leaned closer, his shoulder pressed against the wood plank that separated them.

"Cas, I really want to know about you becoming a king. It sounds so fascinating," she tried again and gave him her most persuasive smile. If she was lucky, she would have better results with him than she had during the past few days with Devon.

"Mr. Heaton says it has somethin' to do with my antecedents—I think that was the word. I've got some relatives named Flora and Charlie that seem to be real important—highly placed, don't you know." Now that he had begun, Casimir seemed content to rattle on about his elevation to king. "Mr. Heaton doesn't care for this man named George, or is it three Georges? I think he mentioned something about George's son, too, but I can't remember exactly. He doesn't like the work this George person is doin', and he thinks I could do a better job."

"Where does this George person live, Cas?" She had to be wrong in what she was thinking. Surely Casimir was not talking about King George, it was too absurd. The king was ill, and the Prince of Wales was Regent now. Her mother's novels never had anything this remarkable in them. If this was his story, it was clear he was more than a little soft in the upper works.

"I think he lives in London 'cause Mr. Heaton says we're going there when he's collected enough money. This son of George's just throws money away, so Mr. Heaton says we'll need our own, and I can have my picture on it." He nodded in satisfaction, looking at Joslyn for some kind of approval. When she remained silent, he asked, "Have you ever been to London? I've always wanted to go, but I never managed to get out of Southampton when we've landed south."

Looking at his eager, open—and totally vacant—face, Joslyn wanted to cry in frustration. This was the only person who could help her escape from Mr. Heaton—a most disheartening prospect. Was there any truth in what he was saying, or was Casimir spinning this fairy tale from his disturbed mind? Perhaps he was a relative of Heaton's and needed to be locked away for his and everyone else's safety. She decided it would be best to humor him for the time being. "Yes, I have been to London, but it was years ago. Who do you usually travel with, Cas? Do you have family?"

"I have an aunt and uncle who raised me after my parents were killed in a hurricane off the Indies. My mother liked to sail with my father whenever she could," Cas confided, then reached through the partition to take Joslyn's hand. He looked deep into her eyes with a sorrowful look that reminded her of Ann-Louise when she needed to be let out of doors. "It's so sad to be an orphan, all alone in the world. My aunt and uncle are more concerned with my cousin

James than me. He's the one that's goin' to inherit the business."

"You are in shipping?" She grasped at any subject that would keep Casimir talking, hoping that she could lead him back to the matter at hand. How could this Heaton be planning to overthrow the government? "You said you arrived on a ship before you met Mr. Heaton?"

"The family's been in shippin' for years, though my father was a privateer durin' the war. That was the Revolution, a real war, not like this silly war of Mr. Madison's that nobody wants. That's how he met my mother when he captured her ship."

"How romantic," Joslyn murmured. She wondered how she was going to get her hand back from the young man without seeming terribly rude. She might have to do something drastic, however, since she did not care for the way he was stroking her fingers.

"My whole family is romantic. If I was at home right now, I'd suggest we turn down the lantern," he announced in a whispering tone with a decided leer, seeming disappointed that her walking dress was buttoned up to her neck. "Not that it would be that romantic without my lyre. I've been told that I play beautifully."

"Would you be able to play when you are king?" She would play his game by asking ridiculous questions, hoping to glean more pertinent information.

"I haven't considered that. I don't rightly know what a king does, but I suppose if I was a king I could do what I wanted." He paused, frowning over the matter. Whatever he was thinking was not terribly pleasant, but it stopped his stroking hand momentarily. "I suppose I'd have to ask Mr. Heaton 'cause he said that he would be there with me, teachin' me how to be king. I think he said somethin' about playin' at being a kingmaker. Must be some English title, we don't have anythin' like that in North Carolina."

Or here in England since the Middle Ages, I think, Joslyn determined. There had been someone called the Kingmaker who met a very nasty end because of his ambition. The general always read her stories of great battles when she was a child, but unfortunately she had not paid much attention at the time. How was she to know that she would be kidnapped when she was grown and need to recall the information?

"What are you doing?" she exclaimed, snatching her hand away from Casimir's grasp and jumping to her feet to get out of his reach. The man had been chewing on her fingers. She was locked up with a lunatic who had delusions of grandeur as well as other considerations she did not want to dwell on.

"I was just kissin' your hand. There's no call to get upset. Why do women in this country always fuss over some gentlemanly attention?" He got to his feet as well and began pacing the length of his cell, as Joslyn was beginning to consider their chambers. "English women are so confusin', lookin' so pretty and makin' a fellow think they might be friendly. It's all a sham 'cause they are just playin', leadin' a fellow to think he might be their beau. I wish I was home with my Elizabeth; she understands me."

"You have a sweetheart named Elizabeth?" Joslyn sighed as she asked the question, wondering where Casimir was going to lead her this time. Wherever it was, she was going to keep a safe distance. The touch of his lips on her fingers had been cold and clammy, nothing like Devon's fleeting kiss yesterday at the Bonnie Prince.

Suddenly she stiffened, ignoring Casimir's rhapsodizing about his Elizabeth, who was no doubt safer all the way across the Atlantic. The Bonnie Prince Inn was named for Prince Charles Edward, the Young Pretender to the English throne. There was a semblance of his likeness on the inn's sign board. He had been in this area during the rebellion of some sixty years past. Was the daring and popular Bonnie Prince Charlie the same as Casimir's Charlie? But what was the other name he had said? It was a woman's name. Fleur? Florenzel? No, that was something to do with the Regent—or was it? Flora, that was the name.

"—I wish I could take some of Mr. Heaton's goods back home with me for Elizabeth. She likes pretty things, and she would like some of the fine linen that Mr. Heat—"

"Heaton's Linens!" Joslyn exclaimed, ruthlessly cutting through Casimir's ramblings. She had seen the sign yesterday on a street near the market, just after she saw Devon. He had entered Heaton's shop with another man. What was going on here? What did Devon have to do with the man who had kidnapped her? Was Mr. Heaton Devon's disagreeable employer?

"Well, I must say, I can't say much for English manners," Casimir said disgustedly, his hands on his hips as he glared at Joslyn's still figure. "I'm glad the Macdonalds decided to leave and go to America where we've learned how to behave. A person just doesn't shout out names while someone else is talkin'. I wish I was home right now."

Flora Macdonald—what was there about that name? Joslyn could not think of why she should know about this woman, but it was terribly important. Somehow Casimir's chance of becoming king had something to do with Flora Macdonald. If she could remember who this woman was, perhaps she could unravel the reason she was kidnapped. Or could she?

"Casimir, I apologize for my outburst, but I have had a very long day." She tried to sound remorseful, but it was difficult. She wanted to reach through the planks of the partition and shake the man so hard his brains would rattle, and possibly he would begin to make sense. Why did she have to be locked up with this dolt when Devon would have been a much more suitable fellow prisoner?

Staring at the sullen face of her companion, she knew that their escape would depend on her resourcefulness. Casimir was dim enough that she could talk him into helping her, but only if she had a plan. She also hoped it did not involve him nibbling on her fingers again. That was even worse than Gervais playing patty-fingers under the table. "I shall let you go back to sleep now. I think I have run out of questions."

"Very well," he agreed, picking up his lantern. Giving her another sullen look, he prepared to return to his corner. "Wart will be in early with breakfast, and then he lets me out for a walk around the garden at the back of the house."

"Goodnight, Casimir," she replied absently, her mind already racing ahead to the next day. She would have to see how things were done before she could devise a workable plan. The walk around the garden seemed to be an ideal opportunity to escape or at least cry for help.

She returned to her cot and curled up under the thin blanket that had been provided. From the coarse feel of the pillow cover under her cheek, Mr. Heaton did not waste any of his fine linen goods on prisoners. A shiver of dread went through her as she wondered how long she was going to be in this dreadful attic with only Casimir as a companion.

She fervently prayed that Devon would come soon to rescue her because continued conversation with the other hostage might affect her brain. Was Devon making plans this very minute? Did he even know that she was gone? Until that moment she was sure that Ann-Louise ran back to the Bonnie Prince to sound the alarm. What if her pet never made it back to the inn? The men could have lied about setting the spaniel loose.

The darkness was feeding her fears. Of course Ann-Louise had reached the inn, and Devon and Margate were anxious to discover where Joslyn had gone. But if Devon worked for Mr. Heaton, would he suspect the man's strange, new occupation of kidnapping—not only kidnapping, but also his absurd plans of making some poor half-wit from America the king? As Joslyn drifted off to sleep, she tried to remember exactly who Flora Macdonald was.

"What is keeping that boy? He has had time to run to London and back in the time he has been gone," Devon complained, still pacing back and forth before the fire. He checked his pocket watch, as he had every five minutes since Tully had gone. After the boy left, Margate had suggested—rather forcefully—that they retire to their room. There had already been enough strange behavior to keep the inn buzzing about the strange gentlemen for the coming months. They had to keep to their usual behavior in case Heaton had a spy at the inn.

"Sit down, lad. You're wearing me out with all this walking, and probably keeping some poor soul beneath us awake with your stomping," Margate commented from his chair that was safely out of Devon's path.

"How did Heaton know I was working with the revenuers? I was so careful," Devon muttered without losing step. Though he was talking about the smugglers, in his mind he could see Joslyn's smiling face. When would he see her again? Would he be able to save her from the villains who had taken her?

"It could have been anyone. We're a suspicious lot in this part of the country and don't take kindly to strangers," the older man put in. "He doesn't necessarily know you are a government man; perhaps this is his way of making a deal. He could have taken the girl to test you. Now be patient, I don't want you worn out before your friend arrives," Margate continued, leaning back in his chair with his feet propped up on Devon's satchel. "Look at Ann-Louise, she's conserving her energy until she's needed again."

Devon only snorted at the older man's attempt at humor. He paused to glare at Ann-Louise, who had made herself at home in the middle of his bed. Then he returned to his pacing, all the while thinking over every second he had spent with Joslyn from the moment he had opened his eyes at the lodge. When they got her back—and he *would* get her away from Heaton's clutches—he would confess to his masquerade. He would tell her exactly who he was. Once her temper cooled—in a few days or perhaps a week—he would also explain his plan for finding her a suitable husband.

A tapping on the door stopped his plans to grovel at Joslyn's feet. Ann-Louise roused herself enough to give a low growl. Devon reached the door in a few quick strides, and yanked it open without asking who was on the other side. The sight of McCrory behind a rather grubby Tully brought him to his senses. He immediately swallowed the angry words that trembled on his lips. With a flick of his wrist, he motioned for the pair to enter.

Once the door was safely closed, Devon gave vent to his

feelings in a harsh whisper. "Where in God's name have you been? The girl was taken over two hours ago. Heaton could have her halfway to the coast by now."

"Our Mr. Heaton was dining with the cream of Manchester society and is now snugly tucked in his bed. We were able to place a man in the stables yesterday. He reported in just before I left with the boy," McCrory answered, seemingly pleased with his news. "The boy found me doing surveillance on the Liverpool road. We knew that some of his men were on the move tonight—they must have been after your young lady."

"Tully," Devon said the name as if he had never heard it before. He looked around for the boy and discovered that he was standing by the bed scratching Ann-Louise behind the ear. At the sound of his name, he looked up, his eyes wide. Devon was surprised to see the boy take a step back, almost as if he was afraid.

"Tully, you have done well tonight, but remember that this is our secret," he began gently and reached into his pocket for some coins. He knew better than to approach the wary child, holding out his offering in front of him instead. "Run along now. We may need your services again tomorrow."

The boy's thin shoulders sagged in relief as his mouth dropped open in astonishment. In the blink of an eye, he snatched up the coins, then scampered toward the door. He was halfway out the door before he remembered the reason for his errand, peering about the rough-hewn wood. "Is the pretty lady coming back, m'lord?"

"Yes, Tully, the pretty lady will be coming back, and I am sure she will want to thank you for your help," Devon assured him. Though the boy seemed satisfied, displaying a ghost of a smile before he disappeared, Devon wished he could believe his own words.

"Don't worry, my friend, we'll have her back in no time," McCrory asserted with a hardy clap on Devon's shoulder. He was a few years younger than Devon and of a slight build. Tonight he was dressed in rough clothing instead of his uniform. In the past few weeks, he and his men had assumed a number of disguises to ferret out information about the guinea smugglers.

"What can Heaton want with the girl? Does he think I shall go merrily on my way if he returns her?" Devon began pacing again, still restless and impatient to do something, anything.

"We won't know until he sends his next message," the dark-haired revenue officer answered honestly. "I have my men watching the house, and nothing is stirring. They've only seen two or three men about over the past few days, so Heaton isn't heavily guarded. Once we find out what he wants, we can easily take the house. We might not be able to prove his money hoarding, but we can arrest him for kidnapping. Even the local constable can't ignore that, after being so uncooperative recently."

"That is a small comfort," Devon muttered. "Joslyn is probably scared out of her wits by now, and we sit here doing nothing."

The sound of laughter met this statement even before the words were out of his mouth. Both Devon and McCrory turned to stare at Margate, who was now almost wheezing to get his breath. After a few minutes, he sat back and wiped tears of mirth from his eyes. "Sorry, lads, it was just too much. Devon, your memory is going soft, and the young miss has only been gone a few hours. She's having the time of her life, if I don't miss my guess. To her mind, this is a true adventure."

Devon surprised his companions by doubling over with laughter after considering the older man's statement. In his concern for Joslyn's safety, he had forgotten about the young lady's temperament. Margate was right about the situation. Joslyn would thrive on the adventure of being kidnapped, once she recovered from her initial fears. If he was not so angry at the villain of the piece, he could almost feel sorry for Heaton.

Dropping into the chair opposite Margate, he signaled for McCrory to join them by the fire. "Margate, you old reprobate, you are absolutely right. She is probably complaining right now about not being able to wear the proper clothing for a kidnapping."

"Where is that wine that Dulcie brought up earlier?" Devon continued, while pulling two cheroots from his pocket and offering one to McCrory. After lighting both cheroots and blowing a satisfying cloud of smoke, he sat back. "Since it is almost dawn, we may as well have a council of war. We shall be ready to move the moment Heaton sends word about Joslyn. If I know my Joslyn, it could be sooner than the gentleman planned."

"And not a word out of either of ya," Wart warned as he prodded his two prisoners down the steep back stairs.

The command was not necessary for Joslyn, since she had not spoken a word since Wart had arrived with breakfast. It would probably be sheer torture for Casimir, she thought with some satisfaction, because he had been whining nonstop about wanting to go home. Resisting the urge to thank Wart, she carefully watched her steps on the narrow, dark stairway. She could even forgive the fact that he had been one of her assailants last night, especially since he had not been the one who had hit her.

The daylight hurt her eyes as she stepped out into the fresh air. A quick look at the disorder around her confirmed her suspicions of Casimir's mental state. The word garden could not be associated with the tangle of dried-up weeds and vines within the high walls at the back of the house. She did not think anything could ever grow in this dreary place.

"Jest take a few turns around the walk. I be right here waitin' fer ya ta get done," Wart instructed. He was short and thin, someone Joslyn was sure she could easily overpower if he was not carrying a weapon. But he did carry a pistol, keeping it in plain sight to remind his prisoners that he was in charge.

Casimir took Joslyn's arm as they moved down the stone steps to the walkway. She used every ounce of restraint to keep from jerking away. Wart looked a little skittish, and she didn't want to make any sudden moves. As they moved farther away from the house, she kept alert, studying every inch of ground and the surrounding walls.

"You see what I mean about Wart? He's not big on talkin', a fairly dreary sort," Casimir whispered, moving unnecessarily close to breathe into Joslyn's ear.

She had other things on her mind besides Casimir's advances. They were walking back to the house now, and she had a clear view of all three stories. There was a shed against the lower floor, built against the wall that surrounded the back of the house. What appeared to be stables were just on the other side. If she could reach the second-story window, it would be possible to climb to the roof of the shed, then clamber over the wall to the other side. All she would have to do was figure out how to get out of the attic prison that Heaton had designed and persuade Casimir to go with her.

The task of persuading Casimir might not be such a hard task, she realized, as she began to listen to his complaints. He was not happy with his situation. Why did he have to lament about his problems so? A tiny voice inside her was crying out for Devon, wondering why he had not appeared, but she was not wringing her hands in despair. If no one was coming to her rescue, she would handle the matter herself.

"I am going to speak to Mr. Heaton immediately about the next ship home. He can find someone else to be king," he continued in the same whining tone she had been hearing since first light. "Surely he must have found someone goin' to North Carolina by now. I've been gone too long, and Elizabeth might do something foolish, like marry my cousin James.

"In fact, I'm beginnin' to wonder if James didn't leave without me on purpose. He must've paid that girl extra to keep me with her all—" He broke off when Joslyn gave a choking noise from beside him. "Beggin' your pardon, Joslyn. That isn't fit for a young lady's ears. I forgot myself."

Joslyn was having trouble restraining her mirth. Casimir was the strangest individual she had ever met. Of course, how like a man to talk of his sweetheart and another type of woman all in one breath. Without ever laying eyes on the man, she thought this Elizabeth might be much better off with Cousin James. If James was going to run the Macdonald family business, he had to be considerably smarter than his cousin. Even an ounce of brains would make him a genius by comparison.

"Ah, there is Mr. Heaton now. I'll take up the matter of my ship without delay," Casimir exclaimed, then abandoned Joslyn to trot toward the back steps where another man had joined Wart. The new arrival was a large man dressed in a coat of blue superfine with excessive padding in the shoulders. A gaudy waistcoat covered his protruding stomach spanned by a heavy watch chain. He was wearing knee breeches, and seemed to have taken whatever padding that was left from his coat and placed it around his calves.

Raising her eyes to his face, Joslyn realized she was somewhat disappointed in her kidnapper. His round, flushed face with a thatch of white hair and side-whiskers made her think of a bakery confection—all pink and white. There was nothing sinister looking about this man, with his round cheeks and squinty eyes.

"My dear young lady, I am so sorry to inconvenience you in this manner, but this is a matter of business that must be conducted," the man called as he walked past a complaining Casimir, ducking to avoid the younger man's wildly gesturing arms.

"Wart, take Mr. Macdonald up to his room. I think he is fatigued," he called over his shoulder, and gave an idle flick of his wrist. His eyes never left Joslyn's face, making it apparent he knew that Wart would obey the order without question. "Now then, we shall go in for a nice spot of tea, and you can tell me all about your friend, Mr. Delane."

Joslyn did not say a word, but gave him a regal nod of her head. She accepted his arm up the steps, then walked sedately in front of him into the house, turning only once for his direction to the sitting room. The room was pleasant and well lit, something she was coming to appreciate after her confinement in the attic rooms. Mr. Heaton seemed to have simple tastes, though there were some touches of opulence in the twisted gold trim of the embroidered pillows on the camelback couch. There were other gold oranaments on the mantel, ornate candlesticks and vases with a large gilded, oval mirror above them.

She settled on the white and beige satin upholstery of the couch, spreading out her skirt as if she were wearing an elaborate ballgown, instead of her second-best kerseymere that she had slept in last night. Mr. Heaton was silent as well, picking up a golden bell to ring it, all the while studying his companion with a slight smile on his thin lips. Almost immediately a woman appeared, pushing a handsome mahogany tea cart that she placed in front of Joslyn on a slight hand signal from Heaton.

"Would you mind doing the honors, my dear? 'Tis always a pleasure to see a lady performing the womanly arts."

She did as he requested, though she felt like tossing the contents of the teapot at his smirking face. How dare he act as if she had arrived for a social call? Perhaps Casimir was not the only lunatic in the house. Mr. Heaton seemed to be under some delusion that she was a willing guest.

"Now, my dear, what can you tell about our friend, Mr. Delane?" Mr. Heaton asked after settling on a chair that Joslyn was not sure would hold his weight.

"Before we begin any lengthy discussion, would it be rude of me to ask who you are, and why you had me kidnapped last night?" She took a sip of tea and pretended to be no more disturbed than if they were discussing the prospect of a storm.

"Ah, kidnapping is such a harsh word. I choose to think of it as if you were a surprise guest," he replied without any show of emotion. "Your Mr. Delane has been asking some interesting questions about me, and I simply took the easiest means of discovering what I could about him."

"Mr. Heaton—you are Mr. Heaton, aren't you? There is little that I can tell you about Devon that would interest you," she returned. Hastily she set down her teacup and saucer when she realized her hand had developed a slight tremor. It was clear that this man was not Devon's employer, and what Casimir was saying could have a grain of truth in it. If that was so, she could be dealing with a madman.

"Far be it from me to contradict a lady, since it is apparent that you are quality, in spite of the fact you are traveling with the young gentleman without a chaperone. Anything you can tell me about Mr. Delane is of interest."

"Oh, I see." She had to think quickly about what to say because she knew that the truth was not sufficient. Heaton must not know that she had only met Devon a few days before, or about his accident. She was not going to be responsible for putting Devon into any further danger from this man. "Well, Devon is an old friend of my family's, and he was visiting us recently, following my father's death, you see. I had not seen him since I was a child, and I blush to say it, I fell in love with him the moment he stepped through the doorway. Unfortunately, I am already promised to my cousin Gervais. An arranged match."

"How sad for you," Heaton exclaimed in a show of sympathy, and pulled his laced-trimmed handkerchief from his sleeve when she dabbed at her eyes with her knuckle.

"Oh, thank you, sir." She snatched at the piece of linen, burying her face in it to hide her sudden smile of satisfaction. The story was sheer fabrication, with a few bits of truth thrown in, but Mr. Heaton did not know what was fact and what was fiction. "You see, sir, it seems that Devon fell in love at the same time that I did; however, he has very few prospects. My cousin Gervais will inherit his father's mill, so my mother insisted that I marry him. Neither Devon nor I could stand to be separated, now that we have met as adults. We are running away together to be married."

"Surely Gretna Green would have been the best place to go?" Mr. Heaton asked, his forehead creased in concern, but Joslyn did not trust the look in his eyes. His expression was too alert, too sharp.

Taking refuge in the handkerchief again, she tried to think of a suitable reply. With a hiccuping sob, she looked up again, giving him her most pleading look. "Devon insisted that I would be shamed to be married over the anvil.

He was determined to do the honorable thing, so he was taking me to his aunt's house. First he had to check with his new employer before he left town."

"Who is his employer?"

The question took her by surprise, not because he asked, but because she did not have an answer. If Heaton did not know about Devon's employer, then was it possible after all that Devon was not a draper in Manchester? "I do not know, sir. He never told me a name."

Heaton rose to his feet, his quiet and quite chilling smile back in place. He took one turn around the room, absently picking up a snuff box from a Pembroke table at the end of the couch. Although he opened the jewel-encrusted lid, he did not take a pinch of the mixture. He snapped the lid closed and without looking up asked, "I suppose it is possible then that your Devon is a revenue man, as I suspected, or possibly worse—a smuggler who is after my goods when they leave port in Liverpool?"

She was not prepared for his question and took refuge in something that had seen her mother in good stead over the years. Joslyn slumped over in what she thought was a very credible faint.

9

JOSLYN tried to keep her breathing slow and measured, as if she were sleeping, but it was difficult with Heaton awkwardly lifting her back onto the couch. She really should have planned better by sliding gracefully onto the couch, instead of falling to the floor. It had been her first fainting spell, so she had not known exactly what to do, and was surprised to discover it was such a complex matter. Once Heaton had her settled on the couch, he moved away.

She could hear him calling to his housekeeper for smelling salts or anything that would revive the troublesome girl. Then he was bellowing for Wart and called another name she could not discern. With a little daring, she opened one eyelid a mere slit to see what was happening. No one was directly in her line of vision, and she did not dare move. What was Heaton planning to do next?

Closing her eye again, she tried to think of what to do when she revived. She could not continue to faint every time she did not want to answer a question. Heaton wanted to know about Devon, and she had told him everything she knew. Would he believe that she truly thought the man was a draper? She had suspected all along that Devon was not what he claimed to be—but was he a revenue officer or a common smuggler?

"Come quickly, woman. The idiot girl has fainted just as the conversation was getting interesting. It seems we have

captured Mr. Delane's fiancée." Heaton's voice was coming nearer again, causing Joslyn to redouble her effort to
appear unconscious.

"I don't have no smellin' salts, so I brung the vinegar,"
a guttural female voice explained very close to Joslyn's
side. "That should brang her 'round with no trouble."

A second later the sour smell of vinegar filled Joslyn's
nostrils. The pungent odor tickled her nose, and there was
no controlling the fit of sneezing that overtook her. Joslyn
sat up, pushing aside the cause of her discomfort. Holding
Heaton's handkerchief to her nose, she tried to control her
breathing. After a few minutes she was able to take a deep,
cleansing breath without the threat of another sneeze.

"What has happened?" she asked as innocently as possible, gazing at Heaton and the housekeeper through tear-
glazed eyes.

"You fainted, my dear, when we were talking about your
betrothed," Heaton explained while giving her a speculative
look, almost waiting for her to succumb to the vapors once
more.

"Oh," was all she managed to say in the best whimpering
tone she could muster. She kept her mouth and nose covered
with the handkerchief, leaving only her eyes to show her
distress over the matter.

"I'm so sorry this has disturbed you so much, my dear. I
really had no idea that Mr. Delane was keeping such
important information from you." Heaton dismissed the
housekeeper with a jerk of his head before offering Joslyn a
hand to assist her to a sitting position. When she was
upright again, he continued. "I think it is time that we both
had a talk with Mr. Delane, don't you?"

"Are you taking me back to the inn? Devon must be so
worried."

"Oh, no, my dear. He knows that you are visiting my
home," Heaton stated smoothly, his smile back in place. "I
took the liberty of leaving him a note last night. Now, you
will write the second note that I promised him, asking him
to come here tonight at eight o'clock."

"But that is hours from now." She did not have to pretend

her distress. The panic she felt was real. How was she going to maintain the pose of an innocent dupe for so long? What if Heaton started questioning her again, and she did not remember what she had said previously? Suppose she blurted out what Casimir had been telling her about kings and kingmakers? Suddenly the prospect of being cooped up with the foolish American in the attic seemed an ideal solution.

"I have a business to run in the building next door and can't have Mr. Delane interrupting my commerce by usurping my time during the day," he explained as if she were as simple as Casimir. "Come, my dear, there is a pen and writing paper over on the secretary. I shall be glad to check your penmanship when you have finished."

Joslyn did not need his warning edge to tell her he wanted her to write only what he told her. There would be no mention of Casimir or the strange talk about a new king. "Oh, thank you. Devon will be so relieved to hear from me," she said demurely as she rose to her feet. "I must have given him quite a scare last night. Perhaps he even thought my cousin Gervais had come after me."

She began composing her note as she walked slowly across the room. There must be a way to warn Devon without letting Heaton know. A loving note from his fiancée might be just the ticket. Devon would certainly think something was amiss if she wrote him a flowery, gushing letter. Taking a seat, she wrote quickly.

My dearest, darling Devon,
I am sorry if my sudden departure has alarmed you. I could not refuse Mr. Heaton's invitation. In fact, he insists that you join us at his home this evening at eight o'clock. I count the minutes and the hours until we are together again.

Your loving betrothed,
Joslyn

She read over the short note with satisfaction before sanding the paper to dry it. Then she handed the paper to

Heaton, who had been standing at her shoulder, not trying to hide the fact he read every word as she wrote them.

"You're a very intelligent young lady, my dear. Now I'm sorry to say you must return upstairs while I have one of my men deliver this charming missive."

She rose to her feet, somehow remembering to curtsy in Dulcie's bobbing manner. When she turned to leave, she was hard-pressed to maintain her composure. The man who had attacked Margate at the lodge and had the nerve to hit her last night was standing in the doorway with Wart a few paces behind him. Though she longed to strike him as she passed, she kept her head. It would not do for her to be anything but the demure young lady. She promised herself, however, that she would make him pay for his actions. The sore spot at the back of her head tingled as she walked down the hallway, Wart shadowing her footsteps.

"Rufus, take this to the Bonnie Prince," she heard Heaton order as she mounted the steps. "It is quite amusing that Delane has chosen such an appropriate place to stay, even in blind ignorance. Tonight I'll be able to tell him exactly how stupid he's been."

His harsh laughter followed Joslyn up the stairs as she climbed back to her prison. The sound sent a shiver down her spine, and she vowed that she would make her escape before Heaton came anywhere near Devon.

"M'lord?" Tully stood hesitantly in the doorway of the parlor, as if he was afraid to enter the room without permission.

"What is it, boy?" Devon called from the window where he had been staring sightlessly across the landscape.

"It's come, m'lord. Bloke came up ta me in the stable, he did. Said ta give ya this." Tully held out a white square of paper in a trembling hand. "Is it 'bout the pretty lady?"

"Let's hope so, son. I don't think his lordship could stand another minute of suspense," McCrory announced from where he lounged on the settee near the fire. "Besides, I'm getting dashed tired of sitting around and waiting for this Heaton bloke."

Devon ignored the officer's teasing comments as he

rushed across the room. He snatched the paper from the boy and broke the seal without hesitation. The sight of a feminine hand gave him pause, but no more than the startling contents of the note. When he groaned, the other men were on their feet immediately.

"What is it, lad? Is the young miss safe?" Margate asked gruffly. He was at Devon's side in a few halting steps, taking the paper from the younger man's loosened grip. After he skimmed the note, he gave out a whistle and handed the paper to McCrory. "You don't think Heaton's let the cat out among the pigeons?"

"Is the pretty lady comin' back, m'lord?"

Tully's tremulous voice snapped Devon out of his daze. He reached down and ruffled the boy's already tousled hair. "She will be coming back tonight, Tully. Go on back to your work, and we shall let you know if we need you again."

"Why such long faces? Isn't this what we were waiting for?" McCrory asked as the boy backed out the door, shutting it firmly behind himself. He read Joslyn's note again, clearly unable to understand his companion's concern. "This appears to be a simple note from your fiancée. Didn't you tell me you were engaged to the girl?"

"It is too complicated to explain now," Devon answered, sharing a commiserating look with Margate. How did he tell the officer that Joslyn did not know he was her betrothed— or his true identity—and have it sound sensible? McCrory would not understand that they might be rescuing an enraged young lady instead of a frightened damsel. "It is nothing you have to worry about. Just go ready your men, Lieutenant. We shall approach the house as soon as it is dark—about half-past six, I would guess. We shall reconnoiter on the west side of the square."

"Very well," McCrory returned. He pulled on his cap and left without another word.

"Do you suppose she really knows?" Margate asked as soon as the other man left the room.

Devon gave a shrug, but he was more concerned than he appeared. It was not simply Joslyn knowing about the engagement that worried him. If Heaton knew the whole truth, there was more danger than he imagined, to Joslyn and to himself.

"Look, Cas, it is very simple. You want to go home, and so do I, but I do not think Mr. Heaton will let us if we simply ask. Are you following me so far?" Joslyn was fast losing her patience with the simple American. Why was this so difficult to understand?

"But why do I have to hit Wart? He seems harmless enough," Casimir asked for the seventh time. "Mr. Heaton won't take kindly to that, and he won't let me be king."

"You have to hit Wart so we can tie him up and escape before Heaton finds out." She said every word distinctly and slowly, hoping that this time some part of it would sink into his pea-sized brain. "If you do this, you can go home to your Elizabeth. You would not want to be king without Elizabeth, would you?"

"I'll do it if you give me a kiss," he decided, a huge grin of delight spreading over his face, apparently not worrying too much about his Elizabeth on the other side of the ocean. But the grin faded as Joslyn groaned and got up from her chair to pace the floor.

What was she going to do with this fool? She certainly did not want to kiss him, but did she really have to? "I shall give you a kiss once we have escaped."

Casimir did not answer immediately. His brow furrowed in concentration, as if he sensed that she was trying to trick him. He must not have realized what she was about, however. "All right, I'll do it. Now when was I supposed to hit him?"

Joslyn warily eyed her new partner. Was Casimir suddenly a little too enthusiastic about his task? It did not matter, she supposed, since it had to be done, and she did not think she could do it alone. "You will stand behind the door when he comes to your room. Take that cuspidor you found and give him a little tap on the head before he sees you."

"A tap on the head," Casimir repeated, acting out his part

with relish. He practiced his swing three times before he was satisfied, looking eagerly at Joslyn for her approval.

"Yes, that is it. Then you tie his hands and feet with the strips of blanket that we are going to make. Once you have tied up Wart, you come and let me out. Is that clear?"

"I tap him on the head and come to let you out. Is that when I get my kiss?"

"No, no, no." Joslyn dropped down on her cot, burying her face in her hands. There were only a few hours left before Wart would bring their dinner. How long would it take for her to teach Casimir what to do? Sitting here whimpering was not going to accomplish anything, she scolded herself. She stood up and squared her shoulders to prepare for another session. "Now, Cas, I want you to fetch your blanket. While we are tearing it into strips, I want you to repeat after me."

Later Joslyn lay on her cot nervously listening for Wart's footsteps. He usually stomped up the stairs, but with Casimir muttering his instructions over and over again, it was hard to distinguish sounds outside their rooms. She hoped he understood what he was going to do by now. She was hoarse from reciting his duties, and there was no time to waste. The bells from the nearby church had struck the hour of six only minutes before.

A new sound reached her ears, and she shushed Casimir. Listening intently she could barely hear Wart's first steps as he began his ascent. She lay perfectly still, trying to discern if he was alone. When she heard only one pair of footsteps, she relaxed a little. Casimir still had to accomplish his deed. Would he be able to do it?

Wart came to her room first, a small show of courtesy that Joslyn could have done without tonight. She remained on her cot with her arm across her eyes, pretending to be asleep. The waiting was agony as she heard him leave her part of the room and walk back down the hallway to Casimir's door. A key scraped in the lock, and the hinges creaked. Joslyn held her breath, waiting to learn what would happen.

The confrontation was over before she realized it. A soft

thud and a groan were followed by Casimir's laugh of triumph. Joslyn sat up, not daring to breathe until her door was unlocked. A minute later Casimir stood in the doorway, grinning from ear to ear.

"Do I get my kiss now?" he asked eagerly as Joslyn jumped up from the cot and skipped across the room.

"Did you tie him up already?" She knew that he had not from his crestfallen look. "Come on, Cas, we have to get him tied up before he becomes conscious again."

Wart lay just inside the door, looking as though he had suddenly decided to take a nap. They pulled him over to Casimir's cot before binding his hands and feet. Joslyn took the last strip of the blanket and tied it across the man's mouth for good measure. It would not do for him to start shouting when they were halfway down the stairs.

The trip down was slow and precarious since they did not dare take a lantern or a candle. Joslyn had the presence of mind to remove her slippers and told Casimir to do the same with his boots. Each creak of the stairs vibrated through her, but no one appeared in the lower hallway. Where were the others? Would they run into them in the yard or on the other side of the wall with freedom a few short steps away?

Shaking off her uneasiness, Joslyn breathed a sigh of relief when they reached the window that overlooked the shed. She signaled to Casimir to remain quiet and for him to open the window. Peering over the banister, she waited for the sound of the window sliding upward. The only sound she heard was a grunt.

When she turned around, Casimir was staring at the window, rubbing his shoulder. She dared a whispered question. "What is the matter?"

"I can't get it to move. Hurt my shoulder," he returned, his voice low but all too audible.

She moved closer and inspected the window frame. Surely someone of Casimir's size could raise the window without any trouble. Then she discovered the problem. The window was nailed shut. They had to find another way out of the house.

Taking a deep breath, she signalled for her companion to

follow her once more. She would go for the back door into the garden and hope there was a ladder in the shed to help them over the wall. If there was no ladder, she would have to devise another plan.

There was no movement from below as she paused on the landing. Everyone must be out or at the front of the house, she thought, taking a step forward onto the last flight of stairs. Casimir was directly behind her and blessedly quiet for once in his life. When she reached the bottom of the stairs, she looked to her right, down the hallway to the sitting room. She could hear voices but could not make out the words or tell how many people were talking.

Joslyn turned back to Casimir and placed a finger to her lips to make sure he remained quiet. Their luck had held so far, and she wanted nothing to spoil it. She signalled for him to go to the other side of the hallway, close to the door. Everything was quiet, almost too quiet for her to open the door without making a sound. She reached for the doorknob and snatched her hand back as it began to move before she could grasp it firmly.

The door opened slowly; first an arm clothed in dark cloth appeared, then a shoulder. She stepped back, straight into Casimir's chest, which caused him to make a woofing sound. Joslyn quickly moved aside, then raised her eyes to the face of the person coming through the door. She stared in astonishment to find a young, dark-haired man grinning at her—a man she had never seen before that moment.

He gave her a quick, two-fingered salute before placing his finger to his lips, as she had done earlier with Casimir. He entered the house quietly, a pistol in one hand, and was followed by three other men, all armed. They positioned themselves on either side of the hallway, moving slowly toward the sitting room. The first man through the door stayed close to Joslyn, bent close and asked, "How many are in the house?"

She raised two fingers of her right hand, then raised the index finger of her left hand and pointed to herself. Biting her lip, she shrugged, hoping he would understand there were two men and a woman, but she was not sure about her figures. She had only seen Heaton, Rufus, and the house-keeper, there could be more. When he nodded in compre-hension, she dared whisper a single word. "Devon?"

He grinned and gestured toward the front door a split second before a sharp rap sounded on the wooden paneling. Heaton's voice could be heard barking out an order. The housekeeper and Rufus came into the hallway. The men waited, not making a sound as Rufus started up the front stairs, and the woman headed for the front door. She let out a shriek the minute she opened the door and was confronted by Devon and Margate, both holding pistols.

Heaton came into view, standing in the doorway of the sitting room. He seemed very calm for a man who had just had two armed men walk into his home. Pulling out his watch, he said, "I believe you are a trifle early, Mr. Delane."

Devon studied him through narrowed eyes, his body rigid. "I found that I missed my fiancée and was too impatient to wait until the appointed hour. I hope I have not inconvenienced you."

"Not at all, not at all, sir." Heaton did not move; he simply stood holding his watch as if waiting for someone to make the next move. It came all too soon with a shout from the upper floor. Joslyn tiptoed forward to get a closer look at what was happening. Surely Devon was not going to let Heaton get away with kidnapping her! How could they all be so calm and civilized? The man beside her seemed to be enjoying himself immensely.

"The bloody girl's gone. So's that half-wit Colonial," Rufus snarled as he came thundering back down the stairs. He apparently did not see Devon and Margate as he made his rapid descent. "Wart's trussed up like a Christmas goose. She can't have got—"

He broke off the minute he stepped into the landing, his view of the new arrivals very clear. Devon took a step toward Heaton. "Mr. Albert Heaton, I arrest you in the King's name on the charge of kidnapping."

His softly spoken words seemed to send the entryway into a frenzy of activity. The housekeeper turned on

Margate, seeming to think the older man was an easy target, as Rufus launched himself down the stairs at Devon. Heaton simply remained still, watching the action as if he were observing a prize fight. The smile that Joslyn was coming to hate curved his thin lips.

"Aren't you going to do something?" she whispered to the man beside her.

"Of course, I just wanted to see what the odds were before we made our move," he explained, then signalled his men forward with a sharp whistle. The appearance of reinforcements galvanized Heaton into action. He turned on his heels and disappeared into the sitting room.

Joslyn scurried into the entry hall after the men, calling out a warning to Devon, who had seen Heaton's retreat. While Devon was distracted, Rufus landed a punch to his jaw that sent him reeling back a few steps. Devon regained his balance quickly, yelling at the dark-haired man to follow Heaton. But Rufus was on him again before he could see if his order had been obeyed.

Joslyn moved forward with tentative steps past the housekeeper, who was finally subdued by two of the mysterious men. The third man was following their leader into the sitting room. Her bare foot struck something on the floor. When she looked down, she discovered one of the pistols, and dropped her slippers to bend and pick it up. As she straightened, Devon saw her for the first time.

"Joslyn, get back—" His words were cut off in a whoosh of sound as Rufus planted his fist in Devon's stomach. Joslyn had had enough of Rufus's handiness with his fists. With calm deliberation, she hefted the barrel of a pistol. The general always told her not to trust an unfamiliar firearm in a fight. She understood his reasoning; however, she did not think it applied to the butt of the gun.

The two men danced in front of her, each landing a punch, but neither of them gaining the advantage. Joslyn put a stop to the fisticuffs with simple efficiency, bringing the butt of the pistol down on the back of Rufus's head. After a momentary sense of satisfaction, she felt a trifle squeamish as the man slumped unconscious to the floor.

Devon stared at the fallen man with a stunned look on his face, then looked up in amazement to meet Joslyn's wide-eyed gaze.

She was not sure which of them moved first, but suddenly she was being crushed against his chest. It seemed like heaven to bury her face in the comforting warmth of his coat and hear the rapid beating of his heart. She could have stood there forever. Devon had other ideas, however, and forced her face from its hiding place by tilting her chin upward with his fingers.

"Are you all right? He did not hurt you?" he asked in a husky whisper. He seemed to be trying to memorize her features as his gaze traveled over every inch of her face.

"I am fine, but I think Margate will need to patch you up again." She reached up tentatively to touch a bruise that was already starting to form on his cheek. "Am I ever going to see you when you are not slightly battered?"

Devon's answer was to bend his head and press his lips against her parted, smiling lips. For a minute Joslyn could not breathe, enthralled by the warmth of his lips, the taste of his kiss. Hesitantly she returned the exciting pressure, her fingers feathering through Devon's hair at his temple.

"I thought you were going to kiss *me*." Casimir's whining exclamation was cut short by a shout from the sitting room. Devon raised his head to glare at the blond-haired young man who seemed to want Joslyn's kisses. Before he could investigate this matter, he had to see to McCrory.

Unfortunately, he was not destined to go to his friend's aid immediately. Another voice broke in from the open door of Heaton's house. "What is going on here? Joslyn, why is this stranger holding you in his arms? I demand that you come here at once."

Devon looked down at Joslyn's astonished face, almost amused at how comical she looked. The lady could knock out a villain with one blow, but she seemed almost terrified of the portly man standing in the doorway. He did not release her, his arms tightening around her slender figure almost instinctively, and looked over her head to meet Margate's speculative look.

"The spotty nephew?" He did not need Margate's nod to confirm that Gervais Hunnycote had arrived. It seemed a fitting end to an evening where he had arrived to rescue his fair damsel, only to discover she had taken care of the matter herself.

10

"MARGATE, who is that man? And who are all these other people?" Gervais demanded, waving his hands about wildly to express his outrage. Finally he shook his fist at the Pendertons' former servant. "You, my man, have quite a bit to answer for in this travesty."

"Delane, I need you. Now!" McCrory's impatient voice from the sitting room interrupted whatever the old man was about to say. Margate looked at Devon and Joslyn, giving them a shrug and a smile of anticipation. He had been handling Gervais Hunnycote since the boy was in short pants and felt no threat from the young man now.

"Delane!"

Devon looked around the crowded hallway, reluctantly releasing his hold on Joslyn before signaling McCrory's men to take away the housekeeper and the unconscious Rufus. "Stay here with Margate, love, while I see what McCrory wants."

He turned on his heels as much to go to aid the revenue officer as to escape from Hunnycote's presence. Gervais had been drinking when he—Devon—had visited the Penderton home last week, so there was a good chance Gervais might not remember that he was Joslyn's Captain Farraday. And it seemed that Joslyn might not have learned his true identity from Heaton after all, since she was not as

137

upset as he had anticipated. Or had she simply forgotten her anger in the happiness of her escape?

Still trying to fathom how she had eluded her captors before his arrival, he crossed the room to McCrory's side. The sight that presented itself quickly captured his attention. Mr. Heaton was no longer the dignified gentleman draper. There was nothing remotely dignified about his rotund body caught halfway out the window. Two cloth bags were wedged in the opening on either side of him.

"It seems that our Mr. Heaton's greed has gotten the better of him. He could not make his rather hasty exit without his precious coins. So we'll be able to bring him up on charges of guinea smuggling as well," McCrory reported with a grin on his narrow face. He indicated the gentleman's posterior with a flourish and leaned back against the wall to pluck one bag from the windowsill. As he jiggled the bag, the unmistakable sound of coins could be heard. "Our problem now is how to get our prisoner out of his, er, shackles."

"Does this mean I don't have to be a king after all and I can go home?"

The whining voice from behind Devon distracted both men from the task at hand. When Devon turned, he was not surprised to see Joslyn standing alongside the blond gentleman who had wanted to kiss her earlier. Having experienced the taste of Joslyn's lips himself, Devon did not blame him. He grimly wondered what had been happening during Joslyn's stay under Heaton's roof.

"Joslyn—" Devon broke off, knowing that nothing he could say would make her leave the room at this point. Besides, she might be of service. She seemed to know the complaining man and might be able to explain this new nonsense. "Joslyn, who is this man? Did he say king?"

"Oh, Casimir, do sit down. We shall take care of you in a moment," she snapped impatiently and gave the young man a stern look before turning back to the men by the window. "I will try to explain what I understand, but I think Mr. Heaton is the only one with the complete story."

"Simply start with this matter of kings," Devon prompted

and crossed his arms to wait patiently, as he was learning to do with his unorthodox betrothed.

"This is Casimir Macdonald, who is an American, but Mr. Heaton has told him some story about making him a king. He had the boy locked up in the attic in the room next to mine. It all has something to do with Bonnie Prince Charlie and a woman named Flora Macdonald," she said clearly, looking back and forth from Devon to McCrory. "I think Casimir must have some connection to the Stuart family; however, I cannot remember who this Flora Macdonald is."

McCrory suddenly muttered something dark and impolite under his breath, standing up straight as a poker. "Beg your pardon, ma'am. We aren't dealing with French sympathizers or common smugglers. We've found us a Jacobite plot." When both Devon and Joslyn looked confused, he went on to explain further. "It's that old wives tale about Flora and the Prince during the Forty-five Rebellion. She's the one who helped him get away after Culloden, disguising Charlie as a girl—a strange-looking female at that. Being that the Prince was known to have a way with the ladies, the rumors started soon after Flora immigrated to the Colonies with her husband."

"The Prince thanked her loyalty the only way he knew how," Devon finished, then immediately cleared his throat at McCrory's raised eyebrows and directed a pointed look at Joslyn.

"Now I remember," she exclaimed, clapping her hands in delight. "Papa read to me about the battle and the prince. He always said the soldiers let the Stuart Pretender escape out of pity. So, Casimir is descended from the Prince and Flora Macdonald through their love child!"

Devon groaned but refused to meet the lieutenant's amused gaze at Joslyn's pronouncement. Some day he would learn that his Joslyn was always going to have one more surprise up her sleeve. "Perhaps we should get Heaton out of the window for the rest of the tale. How could a rational man think to attempt putting a Catholic Stuart on the throne after all these years?"

"But I am a Presbyterian," Casimir announced at the same moment McCrory and Devon took a firm hold on the waistband of Heaton's trousers. They popped the man out of the window opening as neatly as a cork from a bottle.

"Of course, I could not put another Catholic Stuart on the throne," Heaton stated as he brushed himself off and straightened his neckcloth. His eyes gleamed with a feverish light as he looked around at the others. "My father and uncle didn't die in vain when the redcoats set their heads on spikes in front of the Exchange like common felons. They were martyrs to the cause like Holker and Deacon; they taught the rest of us a valuable lesson. Henry VIII made this a Protestant country, no matter what the Stuarts tried to do after him. I would have avenged my family for the indignities placed upon them and ruled with a fair hand in place of those fat German Hanovers."

"Come along, Heaton, it's a long time since Bonnie Prince Charlie rode through the streets of Manchester to the sound of the cheering crowds," McCrory muttered while he shackled the man's wrist in proper irons and prepared to drag him out of the room. "This means you'll have to come with me to Liverpool to take care of this. I can handle smugglers, but you'll have to deal with political uprisings."

"Liverpool? Joslyn, can I have my kiss now so I can go home?" Casimir put in with a hopeful look.

"No, you may not kiss my fiancée," Devon returned with some heat, ignoring his irrational anger. The Colonial's interruption kept Joslyn from questioning McCrory's statement concerning Devon's political influence.

"Oh, Devon, did you like the story I told that horrible Mr. Heaton? He kept asking all sorts of questions about you, and so I told him we were running away to be married," Joslyn stated, giving him a delighted smile over her own cleverness. "When he wanted to know why we did not go to Gretna Green, I told him about Gervais following us." All animation left her face as she remembered her repellent cousin waiting for them in the next room. "Oh, no, Devon, what are we going to do with Gervais?"

"Joslyn, what about me?" Casimir was back to his whining again, petulantly pulling at her sleeve.

"You are going home to your Elizabeth," she stated matter-of-factly, wanting to be rid of her attic companion as quickly as possible. "Mr. McCrory and Devon will take you to Liverpool and find you a ship to America, won't you, Devon?"

"Yes, Joslyn, and I shall also talk to your cousin before I leave. He will not be a problem." At that moment Devon would have promised her anything. Heaton had not known his true identity after all. The betrothal was simply a story that Joslyn had concocted, without realizing she was telling the truth. It might not be a bad idea to fabricate another tale for her cousin. "You must go back to the inn with Margate while I go to Liverpool. We have some official business to finish."

"Yes, that is something I mean to speak to you about. You've been lying to me about being a draper, when you were a revenue officer all along." Joslyn tried to look angry as she linked her arm through his but was having a hard time keeping a smile off her face. Devon had come to rescue her after all, and he had kissed her. "If I had known you were with the government, I could have gone back home and had you handle this odious Captain Farraday for me. Perhaps we could still—"

"Joslyn, we shall talk when I get back," he snapped, ruthlessly cutting through her chatter. Though his luck was still holding, and his disguise was still intact, his feelings of guilt were beginning to mount steadily with every word.

"Very well, Mr. Delane, I am sorry that I have detained you." Joslyn did not have to pretend to pout this time. As they walked into the entry, she flounced away to give Margate a hug of gratitude for his part in the rescue. Let Mr. Devon Delane go on about his important business. It was not for her to mention that if he had told her the truth from the beginning, she might not have been kidnapped.

She held her head high as she walked out into the night on Margate's arm. There was no hesitation in her steps when she heard Devon call her name.

"Joslyn— Damn the girl anyway," he muttered as she disappeared into the night. Turning to the two men who remained behind, he gave a disgruntled sigh. "Macdonald, go out to the coach with McCrory. I shall be along in a moment." He waited until the young man was out of earshot before he turned to face Joslyn's cousin. "Now, Hunnycote, we need to have a few words."

"Well, Cousin, I hope you have had a good night's sleep," Gervais announced late the next morning as Joslyn skipped into the parlor of the Bonnie Prince with Ann-Louise close at her heels. He had been waiting for close to three hours, wondering when the girl would make an appearance. "Must you bring that animal in here?"

"My dear Ann-Louise is a heroine, Gervais." She dropped to her knees to give her pet yet another affectionate hug. Nothing was too good for her splendid companion after what Margate told her last night on the way back to the inn. After giving the spaniel one last pat, she rose to her feet and came to the table. "I am so hungry I could eat everything in sight. You would not believe what awful pap Mr. Heaton served us. I hope Devon has him locked away for a long, long time."

"Cousin, what do you know about this Delane person? I know he says he is a friend of this Captain Farraday, but— Joslyn, are you all right?"

"I— I simply swallowed the wrong way," she answered, putting down the muffin that had caused her to choke. What could Gervais mean about Devon knowing Farraday? Was this something else he had been keeping from her? Was that why he had been so willing to help her?

Then she suddenly realized how foolish she was being. Devon said he would take care of her cousin. What better way to handle the matter than claim friendship to the absent Captain Farraday? It was certainly better than explaining that she had found him unconscious in the road.

"Gervais, please do not start on my going back home. I have made up my mind that I am going to visit Devon's aunt until my birthday."

"Well, that is something that I wanted to talk to you—"

"Please, Gervais, I know your mother has always talked about you and I marrying, but, dear Cousin, I do not want to marry anyone. Please try to understand."

"Yes, I know. That is what I wanted to tell you," he said earnestly, leaning forward with his arms resting on the table. He did not seem to mind that his sleeve was now smeared with marmalade from his plate. "I told Mother that I would find you, to assure everyone that you were safe. Can you imagine my distress last night when I made inquiries at this inn? Why, I must have stopped at every inn between here and Dukinfield. Imagine my horror when the boy in the stables told me that you had gone away and that your brother could not find you. Your brother, when I knew there was no such person. Luckily the urchin remembered Heaton's name so I was able to follow this Delane person and Margate.

"I do not know what I will say to Mother when I return, but I have already told her that I have no wish to marry anyone against her will," he continued, his beady eyes pleading with her. "I shall be glad to stand your friend, but I shall not make you go back home. Not if it will make you unhappy."

"Why, Gervais, you amaze me!" Joslyn abandoned her breakfast of muffins and cold ham at his startling announcement. "Could it be that there is someone else who has taken your fancy?"

"Yes, yes, that is it exactly," he exclaimed with a huge grin on his round, flushed face. For a moment Joslyn wondered if his neckcloth was too tight as his spots were becoming more prominent. "I have met another girl that I, that I— Well, actually, I have not spoken to her yet, or even mentioned her to Mother."

"How marvelous for you, dear Cousin. We really should do something to celebrate this event." Joslyn could not believe her good fortune. All her worry about Gervais had been for naught. The man was in love with someone else and had finally found the backbone to stand up to his mother. It was a shame that they had not had this talk earlier; then she might not have needed to take such drastic measures and run away. If she had not, however, she never would have met Devon.

"Actually, I was talking to the innkeeper earlier today about the sights around Manchester. He says there are some old Roman ruins just north of here." He continued to grin over this tidbit of information, overly proud of his accomplishment. "I thought we might go inspect them while we wait for this Delane person to return from Liverpool. Perhaps we could take a picnic along as well. Delane would not object, would he?"

"Gervais, I do not have to ask his permission to go for a simple picnic," she stated and crossed her fingers under the table for good measure. The memory of her last unauthorized excursion was still fresh in her mind, almost making her reconsider. It was so typical of a man to think only men could make such a decision. After being cooped up in Heaton's attic, the thought of a day in the fresh air was too tempting.

"What picnic would that be, young miss?" Margate asked from the doorway.

Joslyn jumped up from her chair to hug her old friend, excited by the prospect of the excursion, and still grateful for his help in her rescue. "Gervais and I are going to go on a picnic near some Roman ruins that Mr. Gantry mentioned. It will be such fun."

"Don't you want to wait for Mr. Delane? He might be back at any time," the old man put in, giving Gervais a narrow-eyed look, as if he thought something was amiss. The young miss usually avoided her cousin like the plague.

"Nonsense, Margate. Devon is tending to his important government business, and even if he did return this afternoon, we could not start for his aunt's home until the morning." She thought her voice held the right touch of lightheartedness. The old man did not need to know that she was still smarting a little from Devon's suddenly brisk manner the previous night. She could show him that his kiss meant nothing more to her than it apparently did to him.

"Now, miss—"

"Not now, Margate. I need the fresh air after my recent imprisonment. Besides, I plan to quiz my cousin about his new sweetheart." She headed for the door without waiting for a response. "Gervais, go tell Tully to get your rig ready. I shall be down as soon as I fetch my bonnet."

"Never mind, boy. I'll talk to Tully myself," Margate instructed as soon as Joslyn skipped through the door and up the steps. "I have a few things to tell the boy about our adventure last night."

"Ah, Margate, I feel like I have not slept in a week," Devon exclaimed as he stepped through the doorway to the parlor, tossing his cape on the nearest chair. "I think I shall be asleep before my head touches the pillow tonight." He eased down into the wing chair next to the fire, lines of weariness etched into his face. With his last ounce of energy he reached for the bell pull next to the fireplace. "It is a dreary, foggy night out, my friend. I am glad to be settled for the evening. You are more silent than usual, my taciturn friend."

Devon could not help teasing the older man. There was great comfort in knowing that Heaton was safely locked away—though still ranting about his cause—and the mission had come to a satisfactory conclusion. Even the prospect of confessing his true identity to Joslyn did not dim his anticipation of rusticating at his aunt's house. "Does the expectation of a quiet retreat on a country estate hold no allure after the past few days? Where is Joslyn by the way? Was she worn out by her great adventure yesterday?" he asked, suddenly realizing that it was very early in the evening for her to have retired. "It would not surprise me. You would not believe what that fool Macdonald told me . . ." He let the words dwindle away as he began to comprehend that something was wrong. Margate was not letting him perform this soliloquy simply for the pleasure of hearing his voice. "What has she done now?"

"You are quick, lad, I give you that. You knew right away that the miss had managed to stir up trouble again," Margate stated, giving a nod of approval.

"Cousin Gervais?" Devon felt a sudden chill, and the tingling was starting at the back of his neck once more. He should have known better than to leave her behind.

"Right again. She took it into her head to go out on a picnic this afternoon. Seems her cousin had heard of some Roman ruins just north of here." The old man sucked on his unlit pipe for a moment. "He also has conveniently fallen in love with some unknown young lady, and now has no desire to marry his cousin."

"I suppose he rode all the way to Manchester just to make sure she was safe?" Devon did not like the turn of the conversation.

"That's what he says."

"She really was taken in by that story? Damn it." Devon jumped to his feet, dragging a weary hand through his damp hair. All he wanted was a nice hot meal and a warm bed, but as usual his Joslyn had decided otherwise. Why was he in love with the maddening girl? That was the revelation that had come to him in a blinding flash on the road to Liverpool, and it still had him confused, even now when he had the urge to strangle her.

"It wasn't so much that she believed that Banbury tale, but she was angry at a certain person who had gone to Liverpool." Margate seemed to notice that his pipe was out for the first time, and busied himself with the task of relighting it. "She was in a bit of a snit with both of us over not telling her about your mission. Since I escorted her back here, however, she was willing to cry friends with me."

Devon stopped rubbing the back of his neck as a sudden thought occurred to him. He gave the older man a searching look. "Why are you so calm about all this? Joslyn is out there somewhere with that twit Gervais, and you are sitting contentedly before the fire, smoking a pipe. Why?"

"I was the one who went to tell Tully to get the twit's rig ready for the excursion."

"So you have pressed the boy into service again." Devon nodded, still watching the other man with a jaundiced eye. "For some reason you are enjoying having me drag this out of you, and for the life of me I cannot figure out why."

"Simply a way of getting through the waiting, lad," Margate murmured with a ghost of a smile on his face at the younger man's irritation. "By the by, Tully took one of your chestnuts so he would be able to keep up with our runaway pair."

"You are an evil, blackhearted, old—" The opening of the parlor door had Devon swallowing the rest of his words. He spun around, but only Dulcie stood waiting to see why she had been summoned.

"His lordship would like his dinner now, girl, and fetch a full bottle of port as well," Margate instructed when Devon simply stared at the girl. "Send your brother in to us as soon as he returns."

"When did you expect Joslyn back?" Devon snapped the minute the girl shut the door. He did not have an appetite but did not have the initiative to contradict Margate's orders. Since he would undoubtedly be on the road again, possibly within the hour, he knew he would need the nourishment. He had refused McCrory's offer of a meal in his haste to return to Joslyn.

"About two and a half hours ago. It shouldn't be long before the boy returns." He drew on his pipe, expelling a cloud of smoke that spiraled over his head. "I doubt that Gervais is stupid enough to try and travel unfamiliar roads at night, especially with an unwilling passenger in an open carriage."

"Gretna Green?" Devon asked as he dropped back into the chair. There seemed little need to pace tonight. If Margate could relax, then so could he, conserving his energy to give Joslyn the thrashing of her life. It was becoming more and more apparent that she had not been disciplined enough during her childhood.

Giving a harsh laugh, Devon buried his face in his hands. Once he had begun, the humor of the situation kept building until his shoulders were shaking. "Margate, is my entire life going to be like this—one terrifying adventure after another, wondering what torture she has devised for me during every waking moment? Will I never be able to let her out of my sight for more than a minute?"

The old man sat forward on the settee, a grin spreading over his wrinkled face. "So you finally figured it out, have you? No more talk about finding a suitable young man for the young miss before you go on about your business?"

"I am terrified to let her out of my sight even more than the prospect of having her send me to an early grave," Devon admitted with another shaky laugh. "She is a delight and a torment. I found myself wanting to strangle that brainless Macdonald, though Joslyn seemed to treat him like a child. He whined all the way to Liverpool about Joslyn going back on her promise to kiss him if he helped her escape."

"She didn't like the way he was chewing on her fingers," Margate put in, "but she put him straight on the matter."

"If you think that you are going to come anywhere near my estate after we are married, you have seriously under-estimated me, my good man. You probably taught her all her tricks," Devon accused with affection, his smile belying his harsh words. "I probably will only survive the first year of marriage. Joslyn will make a lovely widow, terrorizing the cream of society with her ideas of emulating Madame de Stael."

"She'll settle down after she's a marchioness. It's after the children are grown that you'll have to start worrying again." He was rewarded with an agonizing groan before he continued. "Just pray for boys."

"My family tends to run to girls with a single boy for an heir—"

A quiet scratching on the door preceded Dulcie's return. The sight of Tully following closely on her heels had both men on their feet. The boy was out of breath, but he was smiling as he walked across the room. There was no more hesitancy in his manner as he looked up at Devon.

"I done it, m'lord, jest like Margate said ta." He beamed proudly at his accomplishment.

"Have you eaten, boy?" Devon asked quickly, looking over the boy's small body and his smudged face. "Dulcie, bring another serving quickly. We need to be on the road in a few minutes."

"But, sir—" Both Dulcie and Tully began to protest, but Devon cut them off. "I need Tully's help, and he cannot be in full fettle on an empty stomach. Now go on, girl."

"What's your plan, lad?" Margate asked as he joined the pair at the table.

"I shall take Tully with me in the closed carriage I hired for what I thought would be our journey tomorrow. You will go directly to my aunt's house in the morning," Devon stated between mouthfuls of steak and kidney pie. "If we are not there by the time you arrive, I assure you we will not be close behind."

Dulcie arrived a short while later with Tully's portion, but the boy had already shared Devon's pie. The pair of them split the second pie, devouring the food without tasting it. Devon hastily wiped his mouth and kicked back his chair. As he strolled to the door, he paused as he shrugged into his cloak. He reached into an inner pocket to pull out a folded piece of paper. "Here is a letter for my aunt in case you reach Lorin's Reach before me." He handed the note to Margate.

He was turning to leave when another thought came to him, and a slow grin spread across his face. "Margate, where is Ann-Louise?"

"I sent her along with the young miss, of course."

"You are a very wicked man," Devon stated, but he went out the door laughing, with Tully scampering behind him.

"Gervais, I do not like this place," Joslyn declared, looking around the cold, poorly lit parlor of the inn where Gervais insisted that they stop. The wallpaper was peeling at the ceiling, and the wainscoting had not seen a good wash in months. "The fog is not so thick that we could not find our way back."

"Stop complaining, Cousin, and drink your tea," Gervais ordered, pouring himself another generous portion of wine. "It cost me a pretty penny for the landlord to make that pot of tea, so you had best enjoy it."

Joslyn watched her cousin guzzle down his glass of wine in one long pull. It was his third glass since they arrived, and he was becoming surlier with each glass. Oh, why had she been such a fool to come on this journey? The ruins turned out to be a few rough stones that could have been left behind by anyone. She had let her temper get the best of her again.

Ann-Louise whined from her place at Joslyn's feet. She shushed her pet, hoping that the sound would not set Gervais off again. He had complained about the spaniel during the entire journey. In his present temper, she was not sure what he would do.

"Gervais, I do not want to stay here. Devon has undoubtedly returned from Liverpool by now and is wondering where I have gone." She tried to keep her voice level and soft. Her cousin would surely respond better to reasonable conversation than her temper. She longed to box his ears as she had done when they were children.

"It is a little late to complain now, dear Cousin," Gervais snarled, reaching up to loosen his neckcloth. His face was blotchy and red, in the manner that Margate usually saw him. "If you were so anxious to see this Devon person, then you should have stayed behind."

"If you will not take me back to the Bonnie Prince, I shall go by myself." Joslyn was tired of playing games. She got to her feet, gathering up her bonnet and Ann-Louise's leash. The last person she was going to let dictate to her was her cousin. After hours of trying to be nice to him, her patience was wearing thin. How could she have been so foolish to think Gervais was any different now that he did not want to marry her anymore?

"Sit, Cousin. You are not going anywhere without me," Gervais snapped, rising to his feet. "You see, I do not care if you want to leave, you fool. I cannot believe my high-and-mighty cousin, who has always been too good to marry me, has not figured out the puzzle yet."

He took a few staggering steps toward her, but a growl from Ann-Louise brought him up short. "That animal is not always going to be between us, Joslyn."

"Gervais, what are you saying?" Joslyn knew the answer and realized that she had been an idiot. His declaration of a new love and not wanting to marry her should have made her suspicious. Unfortunately, she was so set on showing Devon that she did not care for his indifferent behavior that she managed to walk straight into another disaster with her eyes wide open.

"I am saying, my dear Cousin, that we are staying here for the night," he explained, though his words were beginning to slur. "Tomorrow morning you will be thoroughly compromised, and you will have to marry me over the anvil in Gretna Green."

11

"TELL me what Joslyn did this afternoon, Tully," Devon asked as soon as the coach was underway. Once the boy had given the coachman the directions, Devon told the man to spring the horses. From the jostling he was experiencing inside the hired coach, it was obvious the man was following his instructions to the letter. Now Devon needed something to occupy his mind until they reached their destination. Wistfully he regretted that his comfortable curricle, broken and useless, was hidden in the woods near the general's lodge.

The boy was preoccupied in exploring the interior of the coach, though it was fairly plain in comparison to the one Devon had specially made in London. This one had calfskin upholstery, slightly worn from use, while he had his done in crimson velvet.

"That bloke tooks her ta see some rocks. Wasn't very happy with them," he stated, pressing his face against the window to watch the road pass by. "Then he stops at the Thistle. Knew he were up ta no good."

"Why is that?" Devon was fascinated by the boy's pleasure in his surroundings as he gave his report. Tully's inquisitive nature was very similar to Joslyn's approach to life. Everything was new and interesting to both her and the boy.

"Only shifty coves goes there. Me uncle says it be a den

of thieves," the boy asserted. Tully could not keep from
running his hands over the smooth leather of the door, his
eyes finding each fixture more exciting than the last. "Will
the coachman knows where ta go?"

"You told him the directions, but you can keep watch out
the window. If he makes a wrong turn, you will know. Then
I shall knock on the ceiling with this." Devon pulled his
pistol from beneath his coat as the boy settled next to him on
the banquette.

"M'lord, what's gonna happen when we finds the pretty
lady?" Tully asked almost in a whisper, his eyes growing
wide as he stared at the pistol.

"I am going to take the pretty lady home with me,"
Devon answered, his mind racing ahead to the isolated inn
that the boy described. As usual, he was torn between anger
and affection as he considered Joslyn's dilemma. Just once
he wished she would do something that was expected. As he
considered the matter, however, he decided that she would
not be Joslyn if she acted in an ordinary fashion. That was
why he had come so quickly to love her, and without
realizing it. The emotion had taken him by surprise, much
as the lady had at their first meeting.

He had never known a woman who could capture his
interest for more than a few weeks. He had joined the army
to do something worthwhile with his life, even if it meant
ending it. He smiled now at the naiveté and impetuousness
of his ambition, but if he had not joined the army, he would
not have met the general. The man had known that Devon
would not be able to resist his daughter for long. But he still
had a major obstacle to his future—Joslyn. Her demand for
independence as well as her hurt pride over her father's will
had made it necessary to hide his identity. How much longer
until he could end this masquerade? His natural impatience
wanted it to be soon, but was Joslyn ready for his confession?

"M'lord, be yer home far away?" Tully asked, still
squirming in his seat, as impatient as Devon to reach their
destination.

"My family has a house in London and a house in

Yorkshire," he answered absently, not bothering to mention the minor farm properties, and he wondered how Joslyn would feel about Ruston's Retreat. The stone fortress had been in the family since the days of Crecy, when his ancestor fought with Edward III and was justly rewarded.

A lusty sigh from his companion drew Devon's attention. "Do not fret, lad. You will be traveling with us to my aunt's house once we find the pretty lady."

"Oh, m'lord," Tully barely managed, making Devon wonder if he would have to fight a duel with the boy to claim his Joslyn's hand.

The thought of fighting for Joslyn made him wonder what lay ahead at the Thistle. Was Gervais the idiot that he appeared to be? He certainly hoped so. There was enough on his conscience in his relationship with the lady without having to harm one of her relatives, no matter how repellent the man was. If Devon was fortunate, his resourceful darling would have the matter well in hand when he arrived.

"Gervais, do not be more of a fool than usual. Devon and Margate will never believe that I let you come near me," Joslyn snapped in answer to her cousin's dramatic announcement. She returned to her seat rather than come to blows with him in his current aggressive mood. Sipping at her tepid tea, she watched him fill his glass once more. With the amount of wine he was imbibing, he would be senseless soon enough.

Unfortunately, she might have worse to contend with if Gervais was not at her side. Even a weasel of a man like her cousin could be useful at times. The man who had greeted them at the inn door had the sinister look she had expected to find in Heaton during her first kidnapping. She choked back an inappropriate laugh. How many people could claim they had been kidnapped more than once and in such a short space of time? It did not matter, except to raise her spirits briefly. At the moment she had to discover more of Gervais's plan.

"Tell me, Cousin, just how do you intend to keep me here for the entire night? Surely someone has already begun to search for us along the road. We did not venture far from our stop at your so-called ruins." She poured herself another cup of tea, since it seemed to be the only refreshment he was going to serve her. It had a slightly acrid taste, but there was nothing else at hand. She certainly was not going to share Gervais's bottle.

"I have a secret for keeping you here. I am not stupid enough to tell you, either." He glared at her across the space of the table that separated them, not looking very happy at the prospect of compromising her. "I am not as stupid as everyone thinks. My mother says I am a fool and cannot think for myself. Well, I can."

"Of course you can, Gervais. After all, you are going to take over your father's business someday, aren't you?" Joslyn realized that dealing with her cousin was similar to conversing with Casimir. Neither man was long on brain power. Would she be able to deflect Gervais's advances as easily as she had Casimir's? She was feeling tired after losing so much sleep in the past few days, but she had to stay alert until Devon arrived.

"You will not have your friend Delane to rescue you this time. The only one who knows where we have gone is the half-wit boy in the stables." Gervais slouched further down in his seat, his triple chins destroying whatever neckcloth design he had attempted that morning.

"Tully? You told Tully where we were going?" This gave her new hope. She smiled as she took another sip of tea. Gervais did not know that the boy only appeared to be stupid because he was shy of strangers and did not speak above a few words at a time.

"Even if this Delane person finds us, it will be too late," Gervais announced with a snarl. His eyes were glittering dangerously, almost like Heaton's before McCrory took him away. Clenching his fists, he rested his forearms on the table. "You will be fast asleep by then."

He sounded so positive that Joslyn was slightly alarmed. Why was he so sure? Was this part of his secret? Then she remembered a valuable piece of information. He was always terrible about keeping secrets when they were children, blurting out whatever anyone wanted to know when he was challenged. Had he changed as he grew older?

"Don't be ridiculous, Gervais. The last thing I am likely to do is fall asleep," she stated with authority, but wished she did not feel so fatigued as she spoke.

"Silly Joslyn, always so superior, always so much smarter than everyone else. We shall shee—see who is the smarter this time." He frowned over his small difficulty in speaking. "You have no say in the matter this time. This is my plan from start to finish."

"Gervais, you are not making the least sense. This secret is just something that you are making up to frighten me," Joslyn continued in the same vein, hoping she was placing the right inflection of apprehension in her voice. She had to discover this secret. Was he planning to hit her? The spot at the base of her head still hurt from Rufus's rough treatment. Glancing to the side, she tried to discover if there was any kind of weapon close at hand.

"I do not hafta—have to make sense, Cousin. I am in charge and can do as I please. Neither you nor my mother can order me around," he stated none too distinctly, his scowl deepening, seeming to need to concentrate on what he was saying. "This is my plan, and it is gonna—going to work. I shall shoe—show my mother that I can do something right."

"I think that you shall be asleep before I am. You are more than a trifle bosky," Joslyn announced, getting to her feet a little unsteadily, much to her surprise. A wave of dizziness made her grasp the back of the chair as she tied Ann-Louise's leash to the spindle. She had to concentrate to walk backward toward the fireplace, moving slowly so Gervais would not notice. The poker leaning against the stonework was the only object she could see that resembled a weapon that would offer her any protection from her cousin.

"I shan't. Nothin' in the wine," he muttered, and grinned as he raised his glass in a salute. Blinking rapidly, he seemed startled to see her so far away.

Joslyn felt better as she moved closer to the fireplace; the movement was helping to clear her head. What had he just said about the wine? *Nothing in the wine.* "You put something in my tea?"

"Ya wernt spose ta guessh," he challenged indistinctly, with the same petulant tone he had always used as a child when he did not get his own way. He started to stand, finally gaining his feet on his third attempt, not having any more control over his body than his speech.

Joslyn backed toward the poker, hoping he could not see what she intended to do. Gervais drugging her tea had to be poetic justice for the laudanum she put in Margate's tea just a few days before. But apparently the dosage he used was not as strong. If she kept moving, perhaps she could stay awake long enough for Gervais to collapse for his overindulgence. She shook her head vigorously, then almost shouted for joy as her heel came in contact with the stone grating of the fireplace. Reaching behind her, she could touch the handle of the poker with her fingertips.

"Wha' ya doin' so far 'way?" he asked, stumbling a little as he started toward her. His expression was almost comical as he looked down to see what he had tripped over and found nothing.

"Taking a little exercise," she returned quickly. Another step backward allowed her to close her hand around the poker. She had to keep talking to distract Gervais. He was twice her size and could easily overpower her. "You really do not want to marry me, Gervais. This is just something that your mother put into your head. She has harped on it for so long that you have begun to believe it."

"Do so," he shot back, and took another step, but his feet did not seem to be cooperating any better than they had on the previous step.

A murmur of voices could be heard outside the door, and Ann-Louise began to growl. Joslyn pulled the poker close to her side, making sure to keep it hidden in her skirts. Gervais seemed to hesitate, listening to the voices in the hallway.

"Toll 'em we din wanna be dis'urbed," he muttered and shook his head, but the movement knocked him off balance. Unfortunately, he stumbled closer to Joslyn and almost within Ann-Louise's range. She strained at her leash, her teeth snapping in anticipation.

"Ya keeps tha aminal quiet." He accompanied the order with a wild kick that was wide of its target. Ann-Louise barked even louder, almost laughing at his failure.

"Gervais, how dare you," Joslyn exclaimed, finally brandishing her weapon in her anger. Gervais lunged at her, grabbing to take the poker away from her. She sidestepped his flailing hands and almost met with disaster as her foot tangled in her skirt. "Don't come any closer, Cousin," she ordered as Ann-Louise supported her with another bark, then grabbed a handful of her skirt to avoid another disaster. "I struck a man last night, and I shall not hesitate to do it again."

They were moving around the room in a bizarre dance, Joslyn noted as she took another step, but Gervais was still between her and the door. The voices in the hall were louder now. Did she dare try to leave the relative safety of the room? Gervais was a minor irritation in comparison to the unknown dangers outside.

"Stop. Movin' too fast. I'll not have—" His words were lost in the sounds of splintering wood, seconds before the door slammed open against the wall. Joslyn made a half-turn to see what had happened, still keeping her cousin in sight.

"Devon!"

Gervais's head snapped up to glare at the intruder, staggering once more as he demanded, "Was gone on 'ere?"

Ann-Louise pulled frantically against her leash, pulling the chair around the floor as she let loose a series of barks that would undoubtedly rouse the entire inn, but Joslyn did not care. She tossed the poker aside and dashed across the room. In her haste, she brushed against her cousin, knocking him off balance. She never noticed as she threw herself into Devon's arms.

"What have you gotten yourself into this time, love?" he asked as his arms closed tightly around her, lifting her off the ground and turning in a full circle.

She did not answer at first, simply content to absorb the feel of his arms, her safe harbor. Tears of relief stung her eyes. She was so tired and had not known how much longer she could have stayed awake. With Devon here, it did not matter anymore.

"So sleepy, Devon, so sleepy, but could not fall asleep until you arrived," she murmured, trying to look up into his face, but it was too much of an effort. Instead she snuggled her head more comfortably into his shoulder, her arms settling around his waist.

"What has he done to you?" Devon asked as Joslyn seemed to melt into his arms. He was torn between holding her and striding across the room to knock her cousin senseless. From the look of the man's gait and the two empty wine bottles on the table, however, Gervais would not be on his feet much longer.

"Jest a shleep powder, nuttin more," Gervais announced before he grabbed at the wall for support, then slid to the floor. He looked around in amazement to discover that he was sitting down.

"I shall deal with you later," Devon promised, then swung Joslyn's limp form into his arms. He gave a sharp whistle that had Tully at the door in a second. "Untie Ann-Louise and bring her along while I take care of Joslyn." He strolled out of the room without a backward glance, still tempted to throttle Gervais. No one challenged him as he carried his fair burden to the coach; he had paid the landlord enough to see to that.

"Oh, sir, what's happened?" Tully exclaimed, his voice cracking as he trotted up behind Devon before he had taken two steps outside the door of the inn. Ann-Louise gave another bark for good measure.

"Don't worry, Tully. She is only asleep," he informed the boy through clenched teeth. Joslyn murmured something that he could not understand, and his arms tightened instinctively around her slender form. "You take Ann-Louise for a quick walk, but do not tarry long. I shall see to our pretty lady."

The dog ran off with the boy as soon as Tully's hand

slackened on the leash. Devon did not spare them a second glance as he continued walking to the coach with his precious burden. If he had not recognized his love earlier, the look of absolute joy on Joslyn's face when he burst into the room would have pierced even his stubborn heart.

As he looked down at her sweet gamine face, he vowed that her cousin would be punished for this night's work. He did not know how he would accomplish it, but something would be done. Perhaps his friend McCrory could lend a hand. For now he had other matters to consider. What had Gervais given her? He had been too distracted to listen to the man's drunken ravings.

Joslyn stirred briefly as Devon carried her into the coach, refusing to relinquish his hold when the coachman offered his help. The man scrambled back to his box at Devon's curt order to leave the moment the boy returned. Sinking down on the banquette, Devon held Joslyn on his lap, telling himself that it would ease the ride if he absorbed the jostling of the coach.

"Be she all right, m'lord?" Tully asked in a whisper as he clambered into the coach with Ann-Louise at his heels. The pair seemed to sense Devon's dark mood as they climbed onto the seat opposite. Ann-Louise laid down with her head on Tully's knees, her eyes trained on her mistress.

"She will be fine," Devon murmured, and smoothed an errant curl away from Joslyn's forehead as the coach lurched forward.

"Devon?" Joslyn's voice was a mere whisper of sound, and he had to bend his head to hear her, his lips brushing her forehead. "It really is you."

"Yes, love, I am here."

"What have you done with Gervais? Or did the wine take care of the matter?" she asked with a weak laugh. "He was so sure he would outlast me."

"What did he give you?" Devon's tone was urgent, hoping she would stay awake long enough to answer. He could see that her eyes were still closed in the dim carriage light.

"Sleeping powder in my tea. So silly of me," she

murmured and began rubbing her cheek against his shoulder. Her left hand clutched at the lapel of his coat. "Gervais is so silly. Wants to marry me. Silly Casimir, too, wanting to kiss me. Everyone wants to marry me or kiss me, except Captain Farraday—even you did, twice."

"Hush, love. Go to sleep now. You are safe," Devon whispered, his heart aching over her ramblings. He wanted to taste her lips more than anything at the moment.

"Cannot sleep. Dangerous without Devon. He will keep me safe."

"Be it a fever?" Tully's question surprised Devon; all his attention had been centered on the woman in his arms.

"No, she is merely talking in her sleep. She has forgotten that she is not at the inn and we have her safe."

"Gervais so silly, and me. Will not marry. Must go to London," Joslyn continued, her voice seeming to grow softer with each word. "Go to London soon."

The coach hit another rut in the road, making Devon wonder how much longer the wretched vehicle would hold together. Joslyn moved restlessly as he held her closer to his chest, his chin resting on her soft curls. It was a long journey to Lorin's Reach. By the time they arrived at their destination, he was sure the coach would be in pieces, much like his heart.

Joslyn was still determined to go to London. Did he have the right to stop her? She was an innocent, but she had proven that she was able to take care of herself. She did not always behave in an orthodox manner, but she was quite capable. How many women did he know who could experience a kidnapping, not to mention two, without becoming hysterical? None but his Joslyn—his resourceful darling. Each time he came to her rescue, she already seemed to have matters well in hand.

He pictured her at Heaton's house wearing the stunned look on her face after she had knocked out Devon's opponent. Then tonight she had taken a valiant stand against her cousin with a poker, all the while trying to stay awake. For a moment he felt a glimmer of hope; she had been waiting for him, or was that simply a part of her drug-induced dreams? He remembered her earlier declaration at the lodge all too well—she considered him in the light of an older brother.

He would not think of his own emotions anymore, he told himself sternly. There was more serious, important business to be considered. When they stopped to change horses, he would send a message to McCrory, who had returned to Manchester to search Heaton's house for more evidence of smuggling. He would have the revenue officer see to Gervais Hunnycote.

If only he could handle his personal affairs in such a satisfactory manner.

Joslyn opened her eyes slowly. Her head was pounding and felt as if it would explode if she moved. As her eyes adjusted to the dim light, she realized she had no idea where she was. Had she succumbed to Gervais's potion in her tea? Was this Gretna Green? Even in the firelight she could discern that this was not the rundown inn where her cousin had taken her.

The furniture was of first quality. The embroidered hangings on the posts of her bed were clean and in good repair. Her hand was resting against something soft and warm. Tentatively flexing her fingers, she began to relax and slowly turned her head. Ann-Louise was laying at her side, her chin resting on her paws, fast asleep. Her loyal pet would not be so quiet if Joslyn was in danger.

A sound from her right caused Joslyn to turn in the direction of the fire. She closed her eyes against the pain as she moved too quickly. Carefully raising her eyelids, she saw a figure slumped in a chair beside the bed. In the flickering light, she smiled at how peaceful, almost child-like, Devon looked in his sleep.

It had not been a dream. Devon had come to her rescue. She smiled and gave a sigh of contentment that roused Ann-Louise for a moment. As she soothed her pet by gently stroking her back, Joslyn wondered where they were. This was not the Bonnie Prince. Unfortunately, trying to think only increased the pounding in her head. She closed her eyes and decided that she would need sleep before facing Devon tomorrow.

Though he looked harmless tonight, tomorrow he would be back in form. Was he terribly angry with her? Would he be reasonable when she made her apologies for her foolishness? He had a right to lecture her this time. If she had not been so childish, Gervais would never have talked her into that *shtupid* picnic. Devon would never believe she was responsible enough to go to London now.

The thought of London brought tears to her eyes. Why did her grand plan make her feel so sad? She tried to capture the reason that seemed to be hidden in the back of her mind, but she was too tired to make the effort.

"Be ya awake then, miss?" a cheerful and familiar voice asked close at hand.

Joslyn did not open her eyes, trying to fathom who was talking to her. Even with her eyes closed, she knew it was daylight. For a moment she was distracted by the realization that her head no longer hurt. Her thoughts were clear, and she was suddenly impatient to get up. Devon had been by her bedside last night.

"Her Ladyship said ta bring ya some chocolate. It'd have ya all right and tight first thing," the cheerful voice continued, causing Joslyn to spring up to a sitting position, rubbing her eyes.

"Dulcie?" Was she at the Bonnie Prince after all? As she looked around, Joslyn knew she had been right last night about her new surroundings. But where was she? And where had Dulcie come from?

"Surprised ta see me, are ya? Tully be here, too," the girl announced as she picked up a breakfast tray from the table near the fireplace. She came toward the bed, then hesitated as Joslyn blinked at her in confusion. "Her Ladyship says yer ta have this in bed. Jest sits back, then I'll set it over ya."

Joslyn did as she was bade, more confused than ever as she settled back against the bank of pillows. Who was Her Ladyship? Dulcie carefully placed the wickerwork tray over

Joslyn's lap, making sure the legs were secure before she stepped back. The chocolate pot and cup and saucer were of a distinctive blue and white pattern that Joslyn immediately recognized. Her mother longed for a Wedgwood tea service for her informal afternoon tea parties.

"Who is Her Ladyship, Dulcie? Where are we, and how did you get here?" Joslyn grimaced at the sound of her hesitant questions. She sounded no better than one of the heroines in Mama's books. They were always breathless and asking silly questions.

"Her Ladyship be Mr. Devon's aunt. She be a right one, though that Margate fella says I has ta be on me best behavior. Told me uncle he'd send me back if I weren't good," Dulcie explained as she poured out Joslyn's chocolate before settling in the chair next to the bed. "He gave me such a lecture, he did."

"Margate? You came here with Margate?" She was beginning to wonder if she was in the midst of a dream. Perhaps Gervais's scheme had worked, and she was sleeping now. This dream is what she had wanted to happen. Not that she would have imagined Dulcie sitting by her bedside, in the same chair where Devon had slept.

"Yes, ma'am. That handsome Mr. Devon took Tully off in a big coach in the middle of the night. He were in a state, he was. Why, he even had Tully sittin' right down at the table with him." The girl clicked her tongue to show her opinion of such behavior, still remembering the man's sharp tone. "Margate told me ya'd be needin' a maid 'cause ya was goin' ta visit a fancy lady. She is that. Toplofty, but she do have a nice smile."

"Her Ladyship?" Joslyn knew she sounded like a half-wit, but her mind did not seem to be functioning very well this morning. Had Devon ever mentioned that his aunt had a title?

If this was a dream, she wanted to wake up at once. She could not face Devon's aunt—Her Ladyship, no less—not after what she had done yesterday. Apologizing to Devon for her stupidity was one thing, but how could she face a stranger with her foolishness? She wanted to slip beneath

the bedcovers and not come out for another ten or twenty
years.

She had had enough adventures for a lifetime. Perhaps
she could sneak belowstairs and find Margate without
anyone seeing her. He would take her back home where it
was safe and familiar. A quiet life in Dukinfield was
beginning to look very appealing.

"Are ya ready ta get up, miss? Her Ladyship set out some
lovely thangs for ya to wear," Dulcie announced, not trying
to hide her excitement. "I wished I had somethin' like this
ta wear fer a handsome gent like Mr. Devon."

Joslyn could plead illness and stay in bed where no one
would bother her. Or would this aunt of Devon's want to
nurse her? There was no way to avoid a meeting. She would
simply have to keep her chin up and hope that she did not
make a complete fool of herself. Why should she be afraid
of a title anyway? Her own mama became Lady Amelia
when her father was knighted. Perhaps Devon's aunt was a
simple lady, not a duchess or a countess. She was probably
worrying for naught.

If I had not run away, I would not be worrying over this,
she scolded herself silently as she swung her legs over the
side of the bed. One look at the lovely cream and pink sprig
muslin that Dulcie was holding made her want to dive under
the bedcovers again. If she survived this visit, she vowed
that she would never leave home again.

"So, you have made me a widow. I shall miss dear Paul."
Lady Joan Lorin picked up her napkin and dabbed at her lips
as she contemplated the very recent, and unexpected,
demise of her husband. She smoothed an errant silver hair
back under her lace cap with a slender hand. "Tell me,
Devon dear, did he suffer much? I do not think I should
want to live if he had a nasty end."

"I am glad to see that you are taking this so well," her
nephew returned calmly from behind his coffee cup. His
lips twitched slightly as his gaze locked with an identical
pair of brown eyes.

His aunt had the Farraday looks, not beautiful but

striking. The Farraday women had always been known for their elegant bone structure and regal carriage. More than one royal lady's nose had been put out of joint by the presence of a Farraday ancestress at court. Lady Joan also had a love of the absurd that his father always claimed came from the distaff side of the family.

"My dear boy, I find this all vastly entertaining. You arrive, barely past dawn, in a hired coach and carrying a perfectly strange young woman across my doorstep. Oh, dear, I really do not know if she is strange, do I?" She raised an inquiring brow at her nephew, but he could not be drawn to comment on the matter. "Where was I? The young woman. You demand a bed for her to sleep off some potion, claiming all the while that you did not give it to her. It was her cousin, I believe?"

Devon nodded, but still did not say a word. He knew his aunt was enjoying herself with her recital and did not want to spoil her fun.

"After we get the young woman settled in my best guest room, you calmly inform me that she is your betrothed. Then you scandalize my housekeeper, poor Mrs. Michaels, by sleeping in a chair all night." Lady Joan paused as the butler came in carrying a fresh pot of hot water. She nibbled on a piece of bacon as the man went about the business of steeping the tea and setting the china pot at her elbow. Leaning her chin in the cradle of her hand, she turned to watch the butler leave the room.

"Now, then, after everyone was settled down again, what should occur? Another strange— No, I really must stop that. A person comes knocking at the door a few hours later inquiring after his young miss," she exclaimed, though calm enough to pour herself another cup of tea and inquiring about Devon's needs. After he demurred, she continued. "He also had brought a young person with him, saying it was the young woman's maid and a sister to the boy that you had in tow. Truly remarkable. Oh, yes, there is the dog as well. How silly of me to have forgotten."

"You are holding up under the strain remarkably well," Devon murmured. He lounged back in his chair with more nonchalance than he was feeling. All he wanted to do was discover if Joslyn was awake yet. Dulcie had gone abovestairs more than fifteen minutes ago. He knew that he needed to stay in his aunt's good graces, however. "Dulcie and Tully work at the inn where we stayed outside Manchester. Joslyn left home rather . . . precipitously, and left her own maid behind."

"Indeed. She also seems to have left most of her luggage behind as well. Fortunately, there are some of Alicia's cloth— Oh, dear, how silly of me? I have no children as well as a dead husband, so I suppose Alicia does not exist. I wonder who those charming dresses belong to then?"

Devon sat forward, leaning his forearms on the table, fully prepared to confess every last detail. After all, he needed to practice confessing. Once Joslyn recovered from her ordeal, he would have to tell her that he was Captain Farraday—or would he? Perhaps it would be too much of a shock this soon. It might be better to wait. "All right, I shall tell you the entire story from beginning to end."

"Oh, no," the lady protested, throwing up her hands in horror at the prospect. "I shall not listen to some dreary, involved story. Your letter has told me everything that I need to know for the present. I think I would rather hear about this adventure from your young lady. Now, how was it you described her? My memory is getting so faulty these days."

He could feel the heat rising to his cheeks as he remembered exactly what he had written. It had been influenced by the euphoria of realizing he was in love for the first time in his life. He mumbled the words, hoping his aunt would let the matter drop.

"What was that, dear? I did not quite understand. If I cannot understand you, how am I going to explain to the servants that you are just the ordinary Mr. Delane on this visit, and not the Marquess of Ruston that they all remember so well?" Her smile was taunting as she waited for his reply, belying her innocent tone.

"I called her 'An enchanting wood nymph with a

penchant for misadventure,'" he finally managed in a groan of despair, burying his face in his hands.

"Men in love are such idiots," she exclaimed with affectionate malice and proceeded to finish her tea. Setting her cup down, she asked in the same innocent tone, "You said I was going to have more visitors, did you not? Something about someone's mother, I think."

12

"Oh, Ann-Louise, I suppose I must go down for luncheon now," Joslyn murmured with great reluctance, stroking her loyal companion's sleek head as she cradled her pet on her lap. She had been sitting curled up in the window seat under the lattice windows for the past hour, trying to find enough courage to go belowstairs to meet Devon's aunt. Dulcie had been running up and down stairs all the while, carrying messages from Margate and Tully and taking Ann-Louise for an outing while Joslyn bathed.

With a sigh of resignation, she set her pet down on the plush pillows and stood up. Her steps dragged across the thick carpet as she approached the cheval glass to inspect her appearance one last time. The cream and rose walking dress fit her admirably, and as did her careless array of curls with a cream ribbon twined in them by Dulcie. Joslyn wished she could muster some enthusiasm for the young woman in the mirror. Instead, she was numb.

A whimper from Ann-Louise caught her attention. The spaniel jumped to the floor and trotted over to her mistress, standing up on her hind legs as if anxious to play.

"So, you think I am being *shtupid* this time, do you?" Joslyn challenged and placed her hand on her hips as she faced the mirror again. She looked over the young woman before her with a critical eye. "You have faced a political fanatic, a brainless Colonial, and your drunken cousin in the space of a few days, not to mention Devon in a flaming temper," she scolded the image, "and now you are letting a woman you have never met scare you half to death. What fustian!"

Ann-Louise barked in agreement, dancing around Joslyn's feet. Her mistress called her to heel, kneeling to give her a stern lecture. "You shall need to be on your best behavior, my dear friend, or you shall be sleeping in Cornwallis' stall tonight."

Satisfied that they were ready for their audience with the great lady, Joslyn walked to the door with her head held high. Her chin began to droop as she approached the stairway, and she hesitated a moment before making her descent. Ann-Louise was impatient and started down the stairs, however, only to stop halfway down when she realized she was alone. She stopped and looked back for her companion.

Joslyn gave a sigh of impatience at being dictated to by an animal, even if Ann-Louise had defended her so staunchly against Gervais. She took one step, then another, which seemed to satisfy her pet. They reached the bottom of the stairs together, where Joslyn stopped again in the center of the entry hall. She did not know where she was supposed to go. There were five doors surrounding the inlaid wood floor. Was Devon accustomed to such a large, elegant house? Fleetingly she wished that he had actually been a draper as she wondered which door led to the sitting room?

"Miss?" The voice coming from behind her had Joslyn swallowing a shriek of surprise. She really needed to gain control of her unsettled emotions, or perhaps Mama's heroines were not such ninnies if people kept sneaking up on them. When she turned, she discovered a gentleman of middle years standing behind her. "I am Casey, ma'am. M'lady would like you to join her and, ah, Mr. Delane in the room to your left. Luncheon will be served within the half-hour."

"Thank you, Casey," Joslyn whispered, but cleared her throat—she was not a coward and could handle the situation. "Ah, Casey, will it be all right if Ann-Louise comes with me? She is very well behaved."

"Just so, miss. I made the young lady's acquaintance earlier, and m'lady is very fond of dogs," he stated without a change in his expression, though she thought she detected a slight curving of his lips. "Will there be anything else, miss?"

"No, no, that is fine, thank you." There was nothing for it but to go into the sitting room. She could not think of anything else to ask Casey to delay the inevitable. Signalling to Ann-Louise, she made it as far as the threshold before she hesitated again.

"Ah, here you are, my dear," a musical voice called from her right. A tall, aristocratic lady rose from the striped green satin settee and walked toward her with her hands stretched out in greeting. "How nice that you are awake at last." She grasped Joslyn's trembling fingers and smiled gently. "Let me look at you. I only had a glimpse of you the night Devon carried you into the house. You have been quite the sleeping beauty."

"It—it is so nice of you to allow me to stay and to provide such lovely clothes," Joslyn managed to say, though her tongue seemed inclined to stick to the roof of her mouth. Even Dulcie's comments had not prepared her for the regal presence of Lady Joan Lorin. Joslyn was sure there was not a queen or a princess who could compare to the striking woman in front of her. Was she supposed to curtsy? She could not remember.

"And this must be the delightful Ann-Louise." To Joslyn's amazement Lady Joan sank to one knee and waited patiently for the spaniel to put out her paw. She laughed in delight as she rose to her feet in a single lithe movement. "Tully was right. She knows how to do a proper handshake.

"Now come, dear, we shall have a little chat before luncheon," she stated, linking her arm through Joslyn's and leading her to the settee before Joslyn had a chance to ask about the boy. "Devon has gone down to the stables to check on his precious chestnuts and shall be back in a minute."

Joslyn sat down obediently, forgetting everything else as she tried to think of what to do with her hands. Finally, she threaded her fingers tightly together in her lap as Ann-Louise settled at her feet. When she looked up at her hostess, she was astonished to discover herself under the regard of soft brown eyes, almost identical to Devon's. She wet her lips and forged ahead. "Lady Joan—"

"Now, none of that, my dear. I shall be your Aunt Joan during your stay. It is so much easier," she requested, her eyes twinkling, almost encouraging her new friend to relax. She coughed delicately behind her hand before she continued. "As Devon must have told you, I have so few visitors that this is a treat."

"Now do not talk Joslyn's ear off. Remember she has had over four and twenty hours of solitude," Devon called from the far end of the room.

Joslyn was on her feet immediately, with a smile trembling on her lips as she watched his tall form stride across the room. He looked very dashing in his riding coat and military-style long boots. She had not remembered his sable hair being so dark or his eyes such a deep brown. A cough from Lady Joan reminded her that she was staring, and she lowered her eyes.

She groaned inwardly, knowing she was behaving like one of those simpering heroines again. This was the same Devon she beat at draughts; the same Devon who shouted at her and criticized her driving skills; and the same Devon who rescued her from her idiot cousin yesterday. Or was it yesterday? What had Devon said? Four and twenty hours?

"Devon, what day is it?" she asked anxiously as he stopped before her. When he seemed about to reach for her hand, she sat down hastily, not sure what she should do. "How long have I been here?"

"This is your second day with us, my dear," Lady Joan put in, patting the young woman comfortingly on the knee. "Devon brought you here near dawn yesterday. You have been sleeping the clock round to recover your strength." She broke off to eye her nephew with an arched brow. "Devon, do not hover so. The girl certainly is not going to come to any harm in my sitting room. Go sit over there. You have had her to yourself for over a week, and now it is my turn. I want to hear all about your adventures, and men always leave out all the interesting details."

"Oh, no. Devon is the one who knows all the details," Joslyn said in a rush of words, hoping to draw attention away from herself. Lady Joan was not as intimidating as she first thought, but she still wanted time to accustom herself to her surroundings. "After all, it is all part of his government work. I still do not know what was done with the horrible Mr. Heaton or if Casimir was able to find a ship back to North Carolina."

"Oh, yes, Devon's government work," Lady Joan murmured, turning to watch her nephew, a slight smile curving her wide mouth. "Do give us all the details about your work, dear boy."

He was going to strangle his best-loved aunt very soon, Devon promised himself as he sat up and leaned his forearms on his thighs. She was enjoying herself immensely at his expense and would continue to do so until he confessed his true identity to Joslyn. The time was not right yet, no matter what his aunt thought on the matter.

He considered not answering his aunt's sally, but for some reason Joslyn looked like a skittish colt ready to bolt. He could not fathom what was bothering the girl, but he would do his best to put her at ease.

"Mr. Heaton is securely behind bars, waiting to be transported to London for trial. He will be tried for guinea smuggling, but not for treason. His scheme to overthrow the government was hardly more than a fantasy. He thought to raise an army by announcing his intentions and displaying his Protestant Stuart to the masses."

"I do not think Casimir would have furthered his cause very much, especially if he let him talk," Joslyn murmured with a laugh, then seemed to remember herself as she glanced at Lady Joan.

"Well, Casimir is happy now, I think. McCrory and I put him on a ship bound for Bermuda," Devon stated, his eyes lingering on Joslyn's downcast face. He had never seen her in this guise of a shy young girl. What was the cause? "He will be able to get transport home from there eventually. It

was the best we could do on such short notice. I am sorry
we could not find him something more suitable."

"You may have saved his poor Elizabeth. She might
marry his cousin James as Casimir suspected, a much better
choice, I think. Most women do not want to marry a man
with the sense of a child," Joslyn returned with a show of
her former spirit. "The man was always complaining about
this and that."

"My dear, that is all men, not just this addlepated
American Devon has told me about," Lady Joan put in
dryly. "You will discover your husband will never be
satisfied with anything you do for him."

"Oh, Devon did not tell you that I do not plan to marry.
I shall be able to claim my inheritance next week after my
birthday, and then I shall set up house in London."

"I see. No, Devon did not tell me," Lady Joan returned,
looking from her nephew to the young woman sitting next
to her with a frown furrowing her brow. "I thought you
were betrothed, or was that part of your adventure?"

Devon wanted to sink into the floor. He had purposely
left out a few details of Joslyn's story, especially the part
about her London plans. Lady Joan was vocal enough about
what he *had* told her. Though she would agree with him
about Joslyn's scheme, he had not wanted to tell her
Joslyn's opinions of marriage.

"I did tell Mr. Heaton that Devon and I were running
away from my family to be married, but I only meant to
keep Devon out of danger," Joslyn assured her hostess. She
seemed determined not to look at Devon, looking at her
hands and her feet, then glancing up to smile weakly at
Lady Joan.

"Is there some reason you do not wish to marry? Have
you never been in love, my dear?" Lady Joan's tone was
gentle and coaxing. Devon found that he was extremely
interested in Joslyn's answer. Was she still dead set against
marriage? He rose to his feet, moving closer to the pair and
leaning casually against the mantel.

"No, I do not think I have ever been in love. It seems
such a silly emotion from what I've heard in the novels that

Mama insists on reading to me," she answered, her voice gathering strength as she spoke. "I wish to have a say in my future and not be dictated to like an ignorant child. Most men seem to think women have no more brains than their horses, possibly less. So I shall be the head of my own household."

"Bravo, my dear. I applaud your integrity and strength of purpose," her hostess exclaimed. Then she leaned forward and stated in a loud whisper, "I think most men think their horses are smarter than most women."

"Aunt Joan!"

"Well, it is true," she declared in answer to Devon's outrage. "Even my dear Paul is—I mean, *was* much more considerate of his cattle. Joslyn, I think you and I shall deal very well together, especially when we send this male off and can have a nice chat."

"Not if I have any say in the matter," Devon muttered, then coughed to mask his words.

"What was that, dear?"

Devon met his aunt's level gaze and knew that she had heard him perfectly. He knew that evil, innocent smile too well. "I said, there is another matter we should discuss— your other guest."

"Oh dear, am I interfering with your plans? I really could go back to Manchester." Joslyn had that hunted look again, and Devon wanted to take her in his arms to comfort her. He took an involuntary step forward, but checked himself after a warning cough from his aunt.

"No, you are not interfering. In fact, it would be dreadful for you to leave with your mother coming to visit," Lady Joan explained. She reached out and cupped Joslyn's chin in her hand, capturing her startled glance. "Am I really such a frightening hostess that you want to run off so soon?"

"Oh, no, Lady—Aunt Joan." She almost tripped over her words in her rush to assure her hostess. "Is Mama truly coming? That would be lovely. Thank you."

"Do not thank me," Lady Joan returned, patting her cheek. "It was Devon's idea. He thought you might like her here for your birthday."

"Oh, Devon, you are too kind."

He was at a loss for words under the warm regard of Joslyn's green eyes. This was the first she had looked directly at him since he had entered the room. Though he found the shy young lady fascinating, he wanted his Joslyn back. He wanted to see that elusive, ridiculously placed dimple when she smiled. "Yes, I seem to remember how kind I have been on a number of occasions."

A flush stained Joslyn's cheeks at his dry tone, apparently remembering some of those moments when he was shouting at the top of his lungs.

"Now that that is settled, let us go in to luncheon." Lady Joan's brisk tone broke the sudden silence. She rose to her feet and signalled for Devon to give her his arm.

"May I take Ann-Louise out on the patio?" Joslyn asked before Devon could move. "She will be much happier there while we eat, and Devon will not sneak her food under the table."

"Go ahead, my dear. We shall wait for you." Devon and Lady Joan watched silently as Joslyn spoke softly to her pet, then lead her to the door. When she was out of earshot, Lady Joan murmured, "You have two days to tell her the truth. If you have not by then, I shall tell her myself. I hate deceiving such a sweet child."

"You have never had that sweet child challenge you with an iron poker," Devon observed, knowing better than to argue. Two days hardly seemed enough time, but then he was not sure two years would be sufficient.

"Do not fret so, my dear. It really is not going to be the ordeal you imagine," his aunt assured him, a strange smile curving her lips as she linked her arm through his. "After all, you are her knight in armor, although slightly rusty because you are perhaps overly fond of your horses."

"Very well, I'll talk to her, but not before her mother arrives," he agreed just before Joslyn returned.

"Devon?" Joslyn's soft inquiry took him by surprise as he blew a puff of smoke into the night sky.

"Over here," he called and tried to find a place to dispose

of his cheroot. After longing for the opportunity all day, he was suddenly very nervous at the prospect of being alone with Joslyn. He knew it was ridiculous, but he was sure he would blurt out a declaration of love the minute she was within his reach.

"Oh, do not put it out. I always enjoyed watching Papa smoke." She smiled at him in the moonlight, no longer the skittish stranger she had been all afternoon.

He remained leaning against the stone balustrade, one foot propped on the stone bench, not sure what to say. Why did she seek him out now after pointedly avoiding him all day? Was she going to talk more about her plans to go to London?

"Devon, about Gervais. You see, I owe you an—" She broke off and looked down at her fingers, fidgeting with the satin ribbons of her blue gown. She took a deep breath and blurted out, "I apologize for going off with Gervais and acting like such a child."

"Was that so bad?" he asked gently, trying not to smile at her petulant look. Did she know that she was the most adorable creature on earth, and that she was turning him into a blithering idiot? He wanted to savor the moment. This might be the last time they would be alone and in harmony. Sometime in the next two days he would have to make his confession.

"Yes, it was terrible, but it was something I had to do." Her smile did not waver as she sat on the bench. "Actually, it was as horrible as I thought it would be. I knew I deserved to have another one of your lectures over this, and you have not said a word."

"I really could not lecture too strongly after the mess I entangled you in with Heaton, not to mention Casimir," Devon answered honestly, taking refuge in his cheroot before he said too much. Would she run away if he said nothing mattered except her joy in seeing him that night, and the way she had rushed into his arms?

"I only shouted so loud that day because I was concerned about you, not because I thought you were foolish, Joslyn. Since I had not told you about Heaton, I did not want you out of my sight." He cleared his throat, wondering if he should continue, then forged ahead. "Margate and I were not sure my curricle accident was due to my work. I suspected it was a plan to rob me and had no connection. With Rufus appearing at the lodge, however, I did not want you in Manchester alone. It turned out you were kidnapped in the one place I thought you were safe."

"No one could have known what that man was going to do," Joslyn said gently. A silence fell between them, Devon smoking his cheroot and Joslyn continuing to play with her ribbons.

"I have been thinking about London quite a bit in the past few days. I think I shall go home and think the matter over a bit more before I decide what I want to do." She turned her face up to stare at the night sky, watching with rapt interest as the clouds drifted over the full moon. "I do know that I shall take steps to contact this Captain Farraday and explain that I really cannot marry him."

"Is marriage that distasteful to you?" He held his breath, almost wishing he had not asked the question and desperately wanting to know her answer.

"No, not really. I know your aunt was joking this afternoon. It's just that I do not know this person and cannot imagine building a new life with a stranger." Her fingers were busy again with her ribbons, though she did not seem aware of what she was doing. "I want to marry someone for love, not because it would be a convenient or advantageous match. After listening to Gervais's and Casimir's strange views of women, I still want a gentleman who will treat me with respect, as if I have some measure of intelligence."

"Perhaps I should tell my friend McCrory that you are not engaged to me. He had a great admiration for your resourcefulness," Devon stated, then wondered what kind of fool he was to mention it. McCrory would be helping to escort Lady Amelia here soon. Why was he throwing the man at Joslyn's head?

"I do not think a man in uniform would be for me. Remember what I told you about military men? Papa loved my mother very much, but he treated her like a pretty doll.

When he wanted to have a serious talk with someone, he turned to me or Margate." Her voice held a tinge of pity for her mother who had missed so much of the man she had married.

What could he say to that? Lady Amelia was not a woman any man would take seriously. Or was Joslyn saying the general made her that way? And how could he explain to Joslyn that he had never seriously considered the full ramifications of having a wife until he met her? In fact, he had not thought to marry until years later.

"Did you realize what a tangle your life would become when you woke up at the lodge that morning, Devon? You have had quite a bit to put up with during the past week."

He grasped at the comment with relief. Did he detect a wistful note in her voice, or was it wishful thinking? "Joslyn, I have to thank you for the most interesting week of my life. In spite of what you might think after our disagreements, I do not think I have ever enjoyed myself so much as during my time with you—and Margate, of course."

"He and Tully are having the time of their lives, telling the staff about their adventures and having Mrs. Michaels spoil them almost as much as Mrs. Ferris caters to Margate at home," Joslyn exclaimed with a nervous laugh. She seemed determined not to look at him. "I think I heard Margate telling Casey that he managed to capture Heaton all by himself. You truly are not sorry, Devon?"

"Truly, Joslyn."

"All right, my dears, it is time to come inside now," Lady Joan called from the French doors of the sitting room. "I have been lax in my duties as a chaperone long enough."

He was going to strangle her, Devon decided, as he ground out his cheroot with the heel of his shoe. Knowing his aunt, he was not sure she had not been listening and selected the most inopportune moment to interrupt. He knew she approved of Joslyn, however, so she was not purposely trying to thwart his poor efforts at courtship.

"I think it is a trifle late for us to worry over the Mrs.

Grundys of the world," he called back, offering his hand to Joslyn and pulling her to her feet.

"Devon, if you want me to learn to behave in a responsible manner, you must be consistent," Joslyn teased him as he tucked her hand in the crook of his elbow. She gave him a ghost of her usual smile as he escorted her into the house.

"Now, if you will both excuse me, I shall retire," Joslyn announced after they joined Lady Joan. "Even after my long nap, I find that I am a little fatigued. Come, Ann-Louise."

"Oh, let her stay with me a little longer," Lady Joan protested, reaching down to pet the spaniel, who was sitting at her feet. "I miss having a dog around since Al— Alain, my poodle . . . yes, my poodle died a few years ago."

"Very well, but as you can see, she is a fickle animal," Joslyn laughed, wondering why her hostess was suddenly glaring at Devon. "Thank you for allowing Devon to bring me here." Impulsively she leaned forward and kissed Lady Joan's cheek. With another fleeting smile at Devon, she left the room.

Dulcie was waiting for her, though she had been dozing by the fire. "Oh, miss, this be the poshest place," the girl exclaimed as she jumped to her feet. "I never guessed that brother of yers were such a rich bloke."

"It was a surprise to me as well," Joslyn returned. She listlessly allowed the girl to unbutton her dress and help her put on her nightgown.

"Wot was that, miss?"

"Nothing, Dulcie," she said and sat down at the dressing table, letting Dulcie brush out her curls. "Have you been enjoying yourself then? Has everyone been treating you well?"

"Oh, yes, miss, but I can't figger something out. There be this fella, some markiss that nobody is 'pose ta mention. It be right queer, 'cause they be talkin' about him all the time in whispers when Mr. Casey's back is turned."

"Perhaps that is Lady Joan's husband. He died recently, I think, since she is reluctant to talk about him as well."

"No, miss, he be an earl. I asked Mrs. Michaels, but that be another strange thing. She says he be in London."

"I am sure that you must have misunderstood," Joslyn stated, and signalled that she was ready to climb into bed. Once Dulcie had her settled under the covers, she sent the girl off for her evening snack with the rest of the staff. Dulcie left, promising to leave the door open a crack for Ann-Louise.

Though she had been tired when she came upstairs, Joslyn discovered her mind was overly active. How she wished that she was as carefree as Dulcie. The girl was impressed by everything around her and half in love with Devon. That did not surprise her. Dulcie was an impressionable girl who would think Devon was the perfect man. She would never worry that he was too wealthy or too well connected because it was all a fantasy to her.

Dulcie had never been on the short end of his temper or had him complain about the way she drove a cart. He had never looked at her with stormy black eyes with his fists clenched at his sides. He never teased her unmercifully or called her an imp. And certainly he never kissed her.

She moved restlessly for a moment, trying to find a comfortable spot on the soft mattress. Of course, he had never kissed Dulcie. Their worlds were poles apart. Devon would never consider a serious relationship with someone so far beneath his touch. He treated her like a younger sister, just as he did Joslyn.

Perhaps she should consider Captain Farraday after all, she decided. They were both from the military set and would understand each other's background. She certainly would never be terrified of meeting any of his relatives. Though she was growing fond of Lady Joan, Joslyn had been on pins and needles most of the day.

Of course, she was only Devon's aunt. What would Devon's mother think if he brought home a girl who had been kidnapped twice in as many days—a girl who had freckles and a tawny complexion from being in the sun without her bonnet? Devon was a man with a future in the government, she was sure. A reckless girl with a penchant for mishaps would not be useful in advancing his career. He deserved someone as poised and as lovely as Lady Joan, who knew how to act properly on every occasion.

A jostling of the bed started Joslyn out of her depressing thoughts. Ann-Louise had come to bed. Joslyn turned to her pet for comfort, wrapping her arms around the squirming spaniel. The dog settled in place with a contented sigh.

"Oh, Ann-Louise, I have done a very foolish thing," Joslyn whispered to her pet, not daring to say the words too loud. "I have fallen in love."

13

"DULCIE, what have I done with Ann-Louise's leash? I have looked everywhere for it," Joslyn asked as she turned up pillows and looked under the chairs near the fire. The spaniel scampered around her, getting in her way, anxious to let her mistress know she was ready for their afternoon walk. That had been their routine for the past three days at Lorin's Reach.

"I think it be in the clothes press," the girl replied and hurried across the room to investigate. The sound of carriage wheels on the gravel of the drive distracted her as she hurried back to Joslyn with the leash. "Oh, looky here, there be visitors, and who be that fine lookin' gentleman riding alongside?"

Ann-Louise spied her leash in Dulcie's hand and began a frenzy of barking. Joslyn grabbed her pet and rose awkwardly to her feet, carrying the squirming animal under her arm as she joined Dulcie at the windows. To gain some peace and quiet, she snapped the spaniel's leash in place and set her on the floor again. The coach door was beginning to open when she finally looked out the window.

"Why, that is Lieutenant McCrory, the revenue officer from Liverpool that helped capture Mr. Heaton. Why is he here?" Joslyn barely asked the question when another familiar figure descended from the coach. "Gervais! How dare he show his face? The man has no sense— Oh."

"Who be the pretty lady?" Dulcie asked when Joslyn suddenly fell quiet.

"That is Mama. I did not expect her this soon," she exclaimed. She turned to run belowstairs and almost tripped over Ann-Louise. Unfortunately, the spaniel felt overly playful and scampered away when Joslyn tried to pick up her leash. "You *shtupid* beast, I do not want to play. Mama is here, and I must go down and meet her. Dulcie, run on the other side of the bed and stop her."

After five minutes of hide and seek, they managed to corner Ann-Louise by the armoire. "Now, young lady," Joslyn scolded as she scooped up her wriggling pet, "you will behave, or I shall lock you in the room for the afternoon." She put her down again, keeping a tight hold on her leash as she checked her appearance in the cheval glass. Would Mama be surprised at how elegant her rackety daughter appeared?

Joslyn hurried down the hall and stairs, Ann-Louise panting beside her. There was no one in the entry hall, but she could hear voices in the sitting room. She was still puzzled by the presence of McCrory and Gervais with Mama. It just did not make sense. Atkins always escorted Mama wherever she went, even on long journeys in a hired coach.

"Oh my, yes, it was so fatiguing," Lady Amelia exclaimed as Joslyn skipped into the room. Lady Joan was handing her mother a cup of tea which the lady accepted gladly. "Oh, my, so lovely. So gracious of you to have me. Things were such a bother at home—"

"Mama, I am so pleased to see you," Joslyn broke in, kneeling at her feet as their hostess excused herself to check with the housekeeper. Lady Amelia obliging leaned forward for her daughter's kiss on her pale cheek. "How was your trip, dear Mama?"

"Oh, Joslyn, take that beast away. You know she sheds on me so," Lady Amelia replied in a distressed voice, almost spilling her tea in her agitation. "I never understood why your father bought you that animal."

"Yes, Mama." Joslyn had trouble keeping her smile at

bay. Dear Mama, who never admitted to sneaking treats to Ann-Louise when no one was looking. She gave her pet the signal to heel, knowing that Ann-Louise would sit quietly at Lady Amelia's feet in hope of earning a bit of cake or a macaroon. "Now tell me about your trip."

"Oh my, such a journey," Lady Amelia began with enthusiasm, since nothing pleased her more than exclaiming over the hazards of travel. "I was bilious the entire time. The swaying affects me so, you remember? Then last night I did not sleep a wink in that dreadful inn. I do not think they aired the bed. It is very possible that I shall come down with influenza, or possibly the ague, from those damp sheets."

"So, you enjoyed yourself immensely," Joslyn exclaimed, not worried about breaking into Lady Amelia's monologue. If she did not, the list of complaints became wearisome for the listeners. "Why are Gervais and Lieutenant McCrory traveling with you, dear Mama?"

"Such a delightful young man, the lieutenant, such pretty manners. Though he is not as good looking as that Captain Farraday," she stated with satisfaction. "I think your father made an excellent choice."

"Mama, when did you see Captain Farraday?" Joslyn sprang away from where she had been resting against Lady Amelia's knee. Had she heard correctly? Was it possible that her reluctant betrothed had finally made an appearance?

"I have just spoken to Mrs. Michaels. Everything is ready for you abovestairs, Amelia," Lady Joan announced from the threshold. "Would you like to go up for a nice rest after your journey?"

"Oh my, yes. I am so fatigued from—"

"But, Mama, what about Captain Farraday?" Joslyn asked in desperation, knowing that nothing would keep Mama from her bed.

"Yes, dear, I shall see you at dinner. I am so happy that we are together again, so happy." Lady Amelia gathered up her reticule and bonnet before giving her daughter a vague smile and joining Lady Joan at the door. "You are so gracious to have us both. I hope that Joslyn has not been a bother. She is such a headstrong girl at times."

"Joslyn has been an absolute joy," Lady Joan replied as they left the room. She looked back over her shoulder at Joslyn's dejected figure and gave her an encouraging smile.

Once they were out of sight, Joslyn gave vent to her feelings. She kicked the footstool and immediately regretted it, forgetting the soft kid of her borrowed slippers. Why had Captain Farraday suddenly made an appearance after all this time? And when had he arrived? Her flight from home seemed to have been timed exactly right.

Since she would not have the answer to that riddle until dinner time, she began to wonder where Gervais and the lieutenant had disappeared. Devon was missing as well. The trio must be together, but why? A whimper from Ann-Louise reminded her that she was supposed to be out of doors. Surely Devon would find her if he needed her for anything, she decided, handily capturing Ann-Louise's leash on the first try this time.

Perhaps if she stayed near the house, she would have a chance of discovering where the men had gone. A walk up and down the drive would be too obvious, but a stroll at the side of the house would be an excellent place.

A half hour later, she was not as happy with her choice. Though Ann-Louise was content, Joslyn had not seen any of her quarry. But the sound of the front door closing as she came around the side of the house raised her spirits.

"So, have you come to gloat over your good fortune, Cousin?" Gervais snapped as he spied her walking toward him. "All that fancy talk about not wanting to marry, when all the while you had yourself a nicely feathered nest all prepared."

"Gervais, have you been drinking again?" Joslyn inquired, unable to understand what he was talking about.

"That is rich. I have been under house arrest since the moment I woke up with that McCrory person standing over me. He poured a bucket of water on me, he did." Gervais was the picture of indignation as he reported the matter.

"Your betrothed set him on me. Treated me like a common felon and made me come here to sign that bloody paper."

"What paper? Gervais, please make sense."

"A confession, that is 'what paper.' His High-and-Mightiness had it all written out, about me taking you to that inn. He says if I ever come near you again, he will take it to the authorities." Gervais curled his lip. His fists were clenched at his side, and his face was becoming red with blotches. "Just because he has a title and money, he thinks he can order people about to do his bidding. It is not right."

"Gervais, you did try to kidnap me," Joslyn said softly, unable to resist the reminder since her cousin was acting so virtuous.

"Oh, you can be so smug now. You were going to be a bloody marchioness. No wonder you turned up your nose at a common mill owner's son—not good enough for you with your fancy lord tucked safely away."

"What lord are you talking about?" She could not have heard him right. "Who was with Devon and McCrory?"

"Oh, you are such an innocent. As if you did not know who this Delane person was all along. And him saying he was a friend of Farraday's and how close they were," he spat out, looking almost as if he would strike her. "Well, it is out of the bag now. All that nonsense about running away, and you were traveling with the man as bold as you please."

"Devon?"

"Yes, Devon," Gervais mimicked before daring to take a step toward her, but thought better of his actions when Ann-Louise growled. "Your fine Captain Farraday, or should I call him by his proper title, the Marquess of Ruston?"

"Oh, no. No!" Joslyn felt as if her cousin had struck her. This could not be true. There was an aching feeling in the pit of her stomach. What a fool she was!

"Well, I shall not wish you joy," Gervais snarled and turned on his heels. He climbed into the waiting coach without a backward glance.

Joslyn watched the coach wheel away without really

seeing it. She was still trying to recover from what Gervais
had revealed to her. Could it be true? Perhaps her cousin
was telling her more lies because he had been brought to
task for his aborted kidnapping.

She had to find Devon immediately, she decided, and ran
to the house with one purpose in mind. The entry was
deserted, as were the sitting room and the study. Where
could he have gone so quickly? Was he hiding from her?

She decided to try the dining room when she realized that
Ann-Louise was shadowing her every move. Hastily she
bent down and unhooked the leash then headed for the
dining room. Devon was not there, but Casey was, putting
away the newly polished silver.

"Casey, have you seen Devon?"

"Oh, His Lordsh— I mean, Mr. Devon has gone to meet
the afternoon mail coach, miss." He looked down at her
with a worried look, knowing he had blundered badly.
"Was there something I can do for you, miss?"

"No, you have done enough, Casey," she murmured,
chewing on her lower lip as she wondered what to do next.
After a moment's consideration, she gave the butler her
most intimidating look. "We have never had this conversation, have we, Casey?"

"Oh, miss, I don't know—" he started, then seemed to
change his mind when she crossed her arms in front of him.
"Yes, miss, as you say."

"I appreciate your discretion, Casey," she managed
through clenched teeth, and spun on her heels. If Devon
was not within her reach, she would wait. It would take
time to plan a suitable revenge for what he had done.

She walked sedately up the stairs and down the hall to her
room, thankful that she met no one along the way. When
she reached her room, however, she gave in to her anger
and slammed the door behind her. Her first instinct was to
pack her few belongings and leave, but that would not
satisfy her sense of outrage. She wanted to confront Devon
with his crime.

"How dare he," she snarled as she threw herself face
down on the bed. "How could I have thought I was in love

with a sneaky, lying, conniving—" She could not think of any other suitable names for the horrible man.

All those lies while he was lecturing her on proper responsible behavior. Just who did he think he was? Did a title give him the right to play with other people's lives? She could not stay still, and jumped up from the bed to pace the room. How could she have been so blind?

Even Dulcie had begun to guess, and Joslyn had told her she had misunderstood. What other lies had she believed? She was the last to discover the truth, since Mama had been talking of Captain Farraday. He had been to their house, but when? Was it before or after their adventures? But surely Margate would have told—

Now she understood Margate's behavior at the lodge. One minute he had lectured her on proper behavior for a young lady, then in the blink of an eye, he was throwing her at the man's head. She would deal with Margate later, after she had finished with Devon.

They had conspired against her, and she had worried that she was not good enough for Devon. He was a snake who did not deserve her consideration. Well, he would see that he should not toy with the affections of Joslyn Penderton.

"Joslyn, is something bothering you? You have been so quiet all through dinner, " Lady Joan said as they walked into the sitting room. The three ladies had dined alone, with no sign of Devon or Lieutenant McCrory.

"I suppose I was missing Devon," she returned, continuing to keep a smile plastered on her face. Her cheeks were beginning to hurt, but she was not going to give away her secret. She did not want anyone to give Devon a warning. "When will he be back? I had hoped to speak with Lieutenant McCrory, but he seems to have disappeared as well."

"I am not sure where they have gotten to by now. Devon was meeting the mail coach and handling some business for me," Lady Joan answered calmly. Joslyn's manner seemed to have reassured her, and she directed Mrs. Michaels to place the tea cart near the fire. "Was there something in particular that you needed?"

"Oh, no. Devon did mention though that Lieutenant McCrory seemed to be more than commonly interested in me." She could not resist the misleading statement, especially since Lady Joan had known of the deceit. She had been willing to play the widow for Devon's sake. "He is a delightful young man, even Mama says so."

"Yes, he is, dear," Lady Amelia agreed from her place across from her hostess. "Very nice-mannered and so considerate."

"What happened to your dislike of men in uniform?" Lady Joan asked as she handed Joslyn her cup. The frown was back in place which gave Joslyn a small sense of satisfaction.

"Well, I have been thinking over the matter of marriage. I am getting a bit old to be so particular," Joslyn answered quickly. She had rehearsed the whole conversation in her room earlier, practicing just the right tone of voice.

"I see."

"Mama, please tell me how you ever got Aunt Verity to leave the house." Joslyn pretended interest, knowing that Mama would ramble on forever about her termagant of a sister. She never stood up to her when she was present, but she could hold forth for hours expressing indignation over every detail once she was gone. With Mama holding court, Joslyn would not have to worry about making a slip, letting the others know she had learned the truth.

Two hours later Joslyn was restless, and Lady Joan was valiantly trying to stay awake as Mama launched into another story of a wretched trip she had taken some ten years past. Devon still had not returned from his mysterious errand.

"Mama, I think it is time to retire," Joslyn stated, ruthlessly cutting into a discourse on the dangers of eating fowl while traveling. "We shall continue this tomorrow."

"Oh my, yes. I did not realize how late it was," Lady Amelia murmured.

"It is no matter," Lady Joan stated with a polite smile.

When she looked at Joslyn in an inquiring manner, Joslyn pretended she did not understand.

"Let me escort you abovestairs, Mama. It is so lovely to have you with me." Joslyn rushed to speak before her hostess could ask her to stay behind. Once they said goodnight, Joslyn bustled her mother out of the room and up the stairs without another word. She would be safely out of sight if Devon came home now. Lady Joan would be able to tell him an interesting tale as well.

The clock in the lower hall struck twelve, and Devon was still not home. Joslyn sat before the fire counting the chimes. After returning to her room, she decided that she would not wait until morning to confront Devon. She would talk to him tonight, the minute he returned. She was ready with her door open so she would hear his arrival. The rest of the household was fast asleep, so she could hear the slightest noise.

A few minutes later she heard the sound of voices coming up the stairs. Impatiently she got to her feet, suddenly nervous about what she must do. As the voices came closer, she walked to the door, peering around it just as Devon came to the top of the stairs. She did not recognize the short, spindly man who was with him.

"Backworth, I know you will take delight in the wretched condition of my clothing. You will be able to make my life miserable—"

"A moment of your time, m'lord." Joslyn's soft words carried easily in the quiet hallway, immobilizing the man she addressed.

Devon turned slowly, signalling the man next to him to wait. "Joslyn, I did not realize anyone was still awake. Did we disturb you?"

"Not at all, m'lord," she answered as she walked toward him. He seemed interested in her mode of dress at this hour, since she was still wearing the pink satin dress she had worn to dinner. "I must apologize for being so impolite during our acquaintance. Since I have had very little experience with the peerage, I did not realize that I was not giving you the proper respect you deserved."

"Joslyn, I do not think we should discuss this now." He looked extremely nervous, especially when she smiled at his uneasiness. "I can explain this whole matter in the morning," he said and began backing away as she kept moving toward him.

"Yes, please explain why you had to lie to me. I am sure the tale is fascinating."

They were almost to his room, and the gentleman he called Backworth opened the door, standing hesitantly on the threshold. His face was a mask of confusion as he looked from Devon to the strange woman.

"Joslyn, please be reasonable." Devon backed into his room with the lady only two steps behind.

"Why should I? I have been lied to, lectured, and generally mistreated for more than a week," she stated with a calm voice that seemed to increase Devon's agitation. "Would you like to explain this to me? Then there is the matter of your conspirators. Does everyone in the entire kingdom know your identity? Or are there a few other half-wits you have chosen as your dupes?"

Devon knew that he should not have had that last glass of wine with McCrory tonight. He was in no condition to deal with Joslyn's fury, if that was what this was. All this time he had anticipated a hysterical, shrieking woman when she learned the truth. But as usual, Joslyn did not do what he expected.

"I had to discover the truth from Gervais. Can you imagine how I felt when that little worm told me what an idiot I have been?"

"M'lord, what should—" Backworth began

"Yes, m'lord. Not only are you that odious Captain Farraday, but you have the gall to have a title as well. I will not have it, do you hear?" Joslyn's voice was starting to increase in volume now, and Devon flinched as he realized that she might wake up the entire household if she continued in her present state.

"Backworth, that will be all for tonight," Devon told his

valet, who was watching with horrified fascination as Joslyn advanced on his employer. For a moment he hesitated, but quickly obeyed when Devon repeated the order.

"His Lordship ordering one of his vassals. What a pretty sight. What orders do you have for me, Your Worship? Is there any little service I can do for you?"

"Joslyn, you have to calm down. It is late, and we are both tired." Perhaps if he reasoned with her, they could get over the rough ground quickly and painlessly, he decided as she backed him into the bedpost, and he knocked his head on the turned wood.

"I shall be gone in the morning. Once I have seen Papa's solicitor in Manchester, I shall go to London as originally planned."

"London? You cannot mean to go through with your plan to emulate Madame de Stael?" Devon had to think of something quickly that would distract her. If he had to tie her up, he was going to make sure that she did not go to London, at least not without him. "You do not—"

"I am a reasonably intelligent adult, in case you have failed to notice." Joslyn gave him a condescending smile, emphasizing her point by poking her index finger in the middle of his chest. "I think I can manage to survive in London without *your* expert guidance."

"You cannot go to London using the example of a well-known courtesan," he snapped, becoming angry at her abuse. He deserved to be chastened, but this had to let up.

"What are you talking about?" Finally he had managed to capture her attention. Joslyn blinked at him in confusion. "Who is a courtesan?"

"Your precious Madame, that is who." Just the thought of Joslyn even considering leaving him was fueling his anger. He knew that his judgment was more than a little impaired by the wine he had consumed, but this was a matter of his happiness, and hers.

"Do not be ridiculous. I shall not listen to anymore— Devon, what are you doing? Put me down," she demanded, trying to wriggle out of his arms, but his hold was too tight.

"I am going to teach you a lesson about your wonderful

life in London, if you go spouting your adulation of
Madame de Stael," he grit out as he stalked over to the
fireplace. Still holding her secure in his arms, he sat down
in the armchair. "Hold still, I am not going to hurt you."

"What are you going to do?" she asked suspiciously,
suddenly going still as she searched his face. Then she
began pushing against his chest.

"Only showing you how a courtesan is treated," he
murmured and bent his head to take her lips. She tried to
move her head, but he snaked his fingers through her curls,
holding her in place. Her lips moved against his, though not
with passion because she was still trying to reason with him.

The sharp crack of a spark in the fireplace brought him to
his senses. Lifting his head, he stared down at the love of
his life, wondering if she would ever speak to him after this
night. He stood up again with her still in his arms and began
walking across the room toward the bed.

"Devon, we should discuss this," Joslyn began tentatively, looking over her shoulder at their destination.

"There is nothing to discuss. I have made up my mind,"
he shot back, never losing a step. He could not keep from
smiling at her distress, knowing that in a few minutes she
would be furious again. He walked past the bed and directly
into his dressing room. Joslyn did not have time to form a
question before he tossed her onto the couch along the side
wall. Then he turned on his heels and walked out.

Joslyn's legs were tangled in her skirt. She was still
struggling to stand up when she heard the door close and the
key turned in the lock. Scrambling to her feet, she ran to the
dressing room door and tested the latch. It would not move.

"Devon, what have you done?"

"The honorable thing, love. Now get some sleep," he
called through the door. "We shall have a nice long talk in
the morning."

Joslyn kicked at the door, and let out a moan of pain. She
had forgotten she was barefoot. Limping back to the couch,
she muttered under her breath. What had gone wrong? How
had she managed to get herself locked in this horrible room?

She lay down, hating Devon and the entire world. She was still cataloging his sins when she fell asleep.

"Good mornin', miss, did ya sleep well?"

Dulcie's cheerful greeting brought Joslyn awake immediately. What was the girl doing in Devon's room? She opened her eyes, only to discover that she was in her own bed. How had she gotten here? She saw she was still dressed in the pink satin when she peeked under the covers, so Devon must have carried her back in the middle of the night.

Sitting up, she rubbed her eyes and was startled when Dulcie placed the breakfast tray over her legs. She blinked at the red rose that lay next to her cup of chocolate. Where had that come from? There was a folded piece of paper next to it with her name in a bold scrawl across the front.

She opened it tentatively, almost afraid to find out what was inside. This morning her anger was gone, replaced by confusion over what had taken place the night before. Why had he locked her in his dressing room?

Joslyn,
Please spare me a moment of your time before breakfast.
If it is convenient, I shall await you in the study.
Devon

Without realizing it, Joslyn picked up the rose, smelling its sweet bouquet. Devon had sent the rose, raiding his aunt's greenhouse. Did he think she would be distracted because she had never received flowers from a gentleman before? Though her temper had cooled, she still wanted an explanation.

"Dulcie, I shall not be having chocolate this morning," Joslyn ordered, putting the tray aside to slip out of bed. Then she realized something was missing. "Where is Ann-Louise?"

"She be down in the kitchen this morning. Margate and Tully have her doin' tricks for the staff."

"I shall wear the blue muslin today," Joslyn ordered and

sat at the dressing table trying to fluff her curls into some semblance of order.

A half hour later she was ready to go belowstairs. Her palms were damp and her heartbeat unsteady. Was she being a fool again? Perhaps she should not wait for Devon's explanation, but begin packing now. She was still uncertain as she stood outside the study door. Devon's deep voice answered her knock immediately.

He stood by a massive mahogany desk, looking as if he had not slept the previous night. How long had he stayed awake in order to carry her back to her room? She could not let the thought soften her resolve. Just as she was about to ask why he wanted to see her, he did the most extraordinary thing.

He knelt at her feet, taking her hand, turning it to press his lips against her palm.

"Devon?" Her voice was a mere thread of sound. She had expected all sorts of posturing and excuses, but never this.

"First I want to humbly beg your pardon," he stated, looking up at her with an uncertain expression, his brown eyes almost sad. "You have every right to be furious with my conduct since we met. Not only have I lied to you, I continually placed you in danger, all due to my arrogance and stupidity."

"Devon, what are you doing?" She wanted to pull away and wanted to stay and listen to his nonsense all at the same time.

"I am trying to tell you that I love you with all my heart," he answered in a husky whisper, seeming to have trouble forming the words. "From this moment, you are free to make your own decision about your future. If you want to go to London, I shall do everything in my power to assist you. But I have another offer that I wish you would consider first."

Joslyn was not sure what she should do. He was telling her that she could do exactly what she had been planning for so long. Yet where was the elation she should feel?

"May I tell you the other offer?" he asked, still holding her hand, his thumb stroking her knuckles.

"Yes, please." It certainly would not hurt to hear what he had to say. If she did not like his offer, then she was free to do as she pleased.

"Please hear me out before you answer," he began, taking hold of her other hand. "I would like to marry you with the understanding that I shall consult you on every matter. I know that you are an intelligent woman who should be treated with respect and not be lied to, even if it is for your benefit. You are also one of the most resourceful women I have ever met, so—"

"Devon, get up, please," she said, not sure if her knees were going to continue to hold her up.

He gave her a curious look, but got to his feet and allowed her to lead him to the settee by the French windows. When they were seated side by side, he asked, "Are you going to consider the offer?"

"I have some questions," Joslyn answered, her voice slightly uneven. She swallowed and tried again. "First, are you asking this because you feel guilty about lying to me and placing me in danger?"

Devon shook his head, somehow managing to capture her hands once more.

"If we tore up my father's will, would it make any difference?"

He shook his head again, and Joslyn thought he had moved closer to her, but she had not seen him move.

"Why did you lock me in your dressing room last night?"

"Because I was afraid I would keep doing this," he announced, a smile curving his lips as he took her in his arms. She did not resist as his lips touched hers or even when he increased the pressure. Then his arms were crushing her against his chest, but she did not even think to escape.

Long minutes later she gasped for air, giving him a wide-eyed look as she asked breathlessly, "Is that what Madame de Stael would expect?"

"Not from me, but you can expect much more," he stated with his usual touch of arrogance, "if you accept my offer."

"Devon, you cannot possibly want to marry a girl who is

constantly getting into trouble." She could not say anything else for the next few minutes because he was kissing her again.

"You also manage to get yourself out of trouble without any help from me. Both times someone tried to take you away from me you had managed to take care of yourself admirably."

"But Devon, you are a marquess." This time she held him off by placing her fingers against his lips, but was slightly distracted as he began kissing each finger. "You must think this through. What would your family say?"

"Exactly what my aunt has been saying since you arrived," he said with a smile. Reaching in his pocket, he pulled something out, but Joslyn could not tell what it was until he slipped something cool on her finger. A sapphire, surrounded by diamonds, winked up at her. "Aunt Joan has been pestering me to marry you almost every hour. Do you think you could put me out of my misery?"

She hesitated for a moment, still uncertain.

"Joslyn, do you love me?" His eyes were filled with an uneasiness she hoped never to see again.

"Yes." There was no hesitation in her answer.

"Yes, what?" he countered, holding her hands against his heart.

She could feel the unsteady beat against her fingertips, and she smiled. "Yes, I love you, and yes, I accept your offer, but on one condition."

Devon pulled back just as he was about to kiss her once more. His eyes narrowed suspiciously before he asked, "What condition?"

"You have to promise to love me more than your horses."

He gave a shout of laughter and wrapped his arms around her. "That is the easiest promise I shall ever make. I cannot imagine having a horse with enticing green eyes and a smile that drives me to distraction. Now may I kiss you?"

"Yes, I am anxious to learn more about what Madame de Stael would expect," Joslyn stated, treading her fingers through his hair to pull his mouth down to hers.

After a very satisfactory interval, Joslyn sat with her head on Devon's shoulder. "Devon, do you have a house in London?"

"Yes, love. I was wondering when that was going to occur to you."

"We can have small parties. And a marchioness would be able to invite whomever she wanted to visit," she began, the idea blossoming as she considered the matter.

"A duchess would have even more power," he said absently, playing with her hand, studying how her ring caught the morning light.

"A duchess?"

"There is one small matter we need to discuss."

Joslyn sat up and turned to look at his expression. He looked like a small child caught in the midst of a prank. "This matter is about a duchess?"

"You see, my father is still alive, but being that I am his oldest son, well, his only son—"

"Devon, are you trying to tell me that some day you are going to be a duke?"

"Not for a very long time, I hope. The family lives at the house at Ruston because Father has never cared for the manor house in Sussex," Devon went on to explain, pulling her down into his arms again. "We shall make some new arrangements now that I am to be married."

"When were you planning to tell me all this?" she asked suspiciously as his lips hovered over hers.

"On our first wedding anniversary, if you had not discovered it by then," he answered, then kept her from answering in the most expedient manner he knew how.

Joslyn decided that this was not the time to argue.

A moving novel of sweeping passion

WINDS OF EDEN
by
Justina Burgess

In the tradition of Barbara Taylor Bradford's
<u>A Woman of Substance</u>

India, at the dawn of the 1800s, is a strange and turbulent place for a young Scottish girl to come of age—but Desiree MacKenzie is captivated by the astonishing beauty of this exotic land. There, her future is threatened by her ruthless guardian uncle. And there her heart is awakened by the love of two remarkable men.   Captain Kirby of the 78th Highlanders vows to love her forever, but it is Hector MacLeod, a successful trader, who valiantly wins her hand in marriage.

Only the test of time will reveal her ultimate fate—from the intrigues of India to the beauty of Scotland and England, from the joys and heartaches of love, friendship, and betrayal, to the bittersweet storms of unexpected change...

A Jove Paperback
On Sale in October